The Rosedale Hoax

Rachel Wyatt

ANANSI 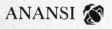   TORONTO

Published with the assistance of the Ontario Arts Council and the Canada Council.

House of Anansi Press Limited
35 Britain Street
Toronto, Canada M5A 1R7

Cover Design: Linda Bucholtz
Cover Photo: Janet Tulloch
Made in Canada

77 78 79 80 81 82   6 5 4 3 2 1

Canadian Cataloguing in Publication Data

Wyatt, Rachel, 1929-
The Rosedale hoax

(Anansi fiction; 37)

ISBN 0-88784-061-2 pa.

I. Title.

PS8595.Y3R68   C813'.5'4   C77-001427-5
PR9199.3.W93R68

for Sally

Part One

On the wall opposite was a picture of Elsa as Miss Niagara Wholesome Fruit 1967. A wide band round her bosom, a Speedo swimsuit to de-emphasize the sexual, a judge on either side of her – men of great local respect – looking with longing at Miss N.W.F. That had been Elsa's triumphant hour.

The singer faded on a last lingering melancholy note and died anti-climactically with a click.

"Do you have to," Bob asked, struggling to push her long hair aside and look at her face, "play those records while we're making love?"

"Guy I met told me about this subconscious learning," she replied.

"It's like having two women at once."

"Lucky you," Elsa murmured, turning her back to him. He was starting to complain. Well he wasn't so fantastic anyway. She had been mistaken in thinking that because he came from Chellow Street, his crummy clothes were the sign of a millionaire's carelessness. Everybody goofed now and then. She just wished she might have been right more often.

Lying in bed beside his mistress, liking the word, wallowing in the soft smell of sex, Bob Ferrand tried not to fall asleep. The dim glow from the red lightbulb lit up the glossy photographs of tall female singers who were well paid for belting out their hackneyed nostalgia in bars lit like the room. There was Jeanie Adams, chanteuse supreme, holding a long-dead bird behind her over both elbows, its improbable feathers trailing to the ground. Frozen with her mouth open, the singer hung there on the wall. Her red dress (an exact copy of which was hanging in the closet by the window), fitted where it touched, which was everywhere. Alongside Jeanie, in a blown-up poster, was the local girl made everywhere (good), who wore her long hair like drapes across her face and peered out to wail of long-lost loves and fast-travelling men she had once known. Popular now, recorded, stamped successful and mailed to Las Vegas, she returned occasionally to honour her home town with a song or two, a flick of her long hair and a glimpse of her broken heart.

"They let me sing two songs tonight," Elsa said, turning back to look at him.

"I was there, remember."

"Was I good?"

"Sensational!"

"Next week they're going to let me wear a black dress instead of the waitress outfit – Mondays and Thursdays."

"That's terrific. You're on your way."

"Mmmmmm." Like a satisfied cat she turned away from him. Her back was soft and well-washed and round and her behind divided like a fresh, fuzzy peach.

The red lightbulb also lit up heaps of discarded underwear. Elsa from Monday to Friday. Dark stockings and red and blue and green panties and bras, none of the sets quite to match as though she was always in a hurry, always behind with the laundry. And she never managed to co-ordinate the colours.

Bob sank back on the bed trying not to let the animal warmth envelop him completely. Soft thoughts of Elsa growing up not far from his home went through his mind like sheep jumping over a rail. When he was eighteen, she was two. She had run through the same fields. Been dwarfed by the same regular rows of trees.

This struggle against sleep was the payment for his early morning pleasure. Was it raining outside? Although the room had outer walls and two windows, Elsa had managed to insulate herself from the world and create an inner room atmosphere of an enclosure within an enclosure, like a harem. The velvet drapes were a sensual addition, the satin covered laundry basket which she never used....But the clock ticked and the pale green phone sat menacingly on the table.

Beside him now, Elsa was sleeping, snoring, totally unaware of him, as she would be if he went away and never returned. The little voice, the awful song, 'I have been looking for you evvvvverywhere', had lured him here. ('I'm not a man who usually goes into bars alone.') Dammit, he had pursued her here with heavy feet and panting breath.

He didn't want to go. Strongly the urge came to him to make a couple of quick phone calls, to the hospital now, to the office later, to tell them he was delayed, held up, had taken the wrong bus, then a wrong connection and was now in a small town two hundred miles north of Sudbury where no one spoke anything but Eskimo, and to snuggle down in the bed for the whole day and the following night. Any foreign movie script would have him buried in the blankets by now, casting care aside and letting the consequences catch up with him later.

If sleep were to overcome him now, how long would it be before police cars were combing the area for him, before Mercer was making statements to the press about the present pressure in the business and before they earned the right to take him, when found, to a psychiatrist? How much free time does a man actually have? "I have to go back home," he whispered but she didn't answer. He got up and dressed. He spread her hair out on the pillow. It would be midday before she woke.

He never brought the car. It would have been a piece of damning evidence and besides the duplex garage was always full. The walk home gave him fifteen minutes of solitude to recall his marriage and remember his family, so that by the time he reached Chellow Street he felt like a soiled and unreliable man.

He skipped along the hopscotch squares drawn on the sidewalk by yesterday's children; feet together on number one, feet apart on two and three, feet together, feet apart. He looked round for a pebble to throw, to play the game properly, proud that a man of his age returning from a night of passion – well they had made love once anyway – could have so much energy. If he was being watched, let them watch. He jumped down heavily on number one again, feet together, and a sharp pain jabbed through his left ankle.

Damn! He leaned up against the Moxford's wall, wincing, and smiling as he recalled his lover in the crumpled bed. Before leaving, at 5:31, he had arranged her hair on the red pillow like dark rays spread out from her sleeping face, the sun.

The sun itself had hit Chellow Street now, reflecting off the narrow shoulders of an early starling and bouncing off the damp patches on the ground. It would be shining too, intrusively, into the hospital to remind Martha, after her hectic and bloody night, that in two hours she could return home.

Bob turned again, dancing a slow waltz, putting no weight on his injured foot, enjoying the silence of the street, alone, returning from his love. Not wanting yet to go inside, into the house where the scent of Martha hung in every corner and would remind him again that he was a guilty man, he sat for a moment on the low wall that protected his lawn from predatory passers-by, short-cutters, dogs. A warbler was singing, the sparrows were twittering, in the ravine a bluejay screeched; all of them waiting for the people of Chellow Street to get up and spread birdseed out for them.

The sun was now established in the sky. There was no question of it slipping back over the horizon. It was shedding its rays on to the collector panels of solar-heated houses, on to the shiny sky-scrapers downtown and on to the other side of the street. It was the cream of the morning and should have been the sole prerogative of returning lovers. But the disc-jockeys were about. Newsreaders were sorting through the stories

6

that must be told. Miners, not singing, were already down their dark, daily holes. On the peninsula, farmers would be weighing up the day as good or bad for picking cherries, for ripening peaches, for spraying the young grapes.

But at number twenty-five, somebody was up and stirring. The black limousine which had been parked outside the house on his first return from Elsa's, was there again. The Reverend Cline had early visitors.

Across the end of the street, the Quinn house stood wide and deep. Inside it, the young maiden, safe within her steely, see-through bubble of insanity, safe from marauders and dragons and Robert Ferrand, watched and waited. He looked up at the tower window. Surely she was there. Martha, years ago, had watched by the window. And the Quinn girl, lacking Martha's attachment to reality, must dream there too.

He was standing on the doorstep, reaching for his key, listening to the faint click-click-click of Harris Soper's insect catcher, his latest, most lethal prototype, when there was a low, bloodcurdling and inhuman screech. Another little animal had put its paw on the unguarded coil. Another murder committed. Finally, the Paper Boy?

'Mr. Ferrand, on the morning of July fifth, nineteen hundred and seventy-six...'

'Martha, I never saw that woman before in my life.'

'On bended knee, Elsa, I am asking you to be my lawful wedded alibi.'

'I put it to you that this innocent child...'

'This "innocent child" is a grown man, your honour, a father of children, nay a grandfather of grandchildren....'

Meanwhile the children slept. They were too old now to come looking for 'Daddy' in the night. He was in fact no longer 'Daddy', but 'Father' sometimes, 'You' often, and 'Him' in their private conversations. Sam might cry out, disturbed by nightmares in which his father, the villain, chased innocent people with balloons which turned into mushroom clouds. And for Dori, there were, no doubt, dreams of childish love, herself in long and glamorous clothes accompanied everywhere by a bearded, handsome youth, name so far unknown. In her pleasant dreams, along tree-lined avenues, she searched for him.

There was a flurry of voices. Bob stepped further into the porch which shielded him. Busy footsteps were crossing the road from the Cline's to the Soper's. The footsteps returned. No sign yet of ambulance or hearse. A whisper or two. The sound of digging. It was not his body. Not his crime.

The morning paper thudded onto the step as soon as he closed the door. The bastard had caught him again.

Giving the Paper Boy time to move away, Bob got the paper in and sat on the hall steps to read it.... 'There could be enormous consequences if the seventeen boxes of secret papers fell into the wrong hands and the minister said when asked that though he personally had not read the entire contents which would be the equivalent to reading *War and Peace* twice, he could say with some assurance that...' Bob's head fell forward, his body sagged. When his forehead hit the tiled hall floor, he came to and crawled into the kitchen to wait for Martha.

He had been dozing off. When he looked up, the vague, numberless clock, an unfinished grade seven project of Sam's, was hinting that it might be ten to eight. Beside it, a piece of polished driftwood, carved too by Sam, proclaimed this to be "Martha's Kitchen".

It was a comfortable kitchen and Martha a good woman. Why then were his feet straying along other paths at uncomfortable hours to Elsa's place? He looked at his feet in reproach.

The thing you had to remember about Martha was that

she'd lived all her life in an atmosphere of money and nice people and good food but with the misfortune to have grown up in the wartime aftermath of noblesse oblige. The cries of the afflicted had been heard by the privileged and their response had left as many casualties in areas like this as an air raid might have done had Hitler possessed longer range bombers.

She and her friends had only played tennis in order to keep themselves fit. They had found no time to read irrelevant books. And she had marched out of these environs with the other crusaders abandoning, with them, comfort for usefulness.

It had all been part of a lemming-like repayment of lives, a return for the young men who had gone away and died. It was a confused and bloody kind of reasoning which had never been clear to Bob, a mere peach-picker from Niagara where the weather was always more important than any other thing and where a man's worth might well be measured in his fertilizer value if buried in the ground.

So she and her friends had spread out into hospitals and foreign fields and parliaments provincial and federal ("I want to be where the decisions are made. That's where I can do most good."), their shining armour emblazoned with the crests and ethics of their summer camps.

They were a fine group of people and Martha was one of them. She, unlike many of them had turned down chances to become an official, a person with a title, a medical officer of this or that, and had stayed faithful to that primary ideal.

They had endurable qualities, like loyalty. It was this in her that he admired so much. A kind of loyalty and truthfulness applied to living. And it had made him say to Elsa Kwan last night at a moment when he should have been totally involved, 'My wife is a very fine woman.'

They, Martha and her former friends, admired fine and endurable things. They knew quality the instant they saw it. A Grecian urn meant something to them. And he, the peasant interloper, was, as it were, spitting in the presence of a Rembrandt.

These thoughts, as he fried the bacon for her breakfast, made his stomach queasy and turned the egg into a near-lethal weapon.

Crud! Why all this soul-searching? Weren't they adults in an adult age? Guilt was for Roman Catholics and they had been taught how to deal with it. Marriages were made in St. Matthew's Church and were therefore permanent. Shared love is doubled love? What the heart doesn't know it can't throw back at you in time of stress. Cliché time on Chellow Street! Elsa was great in bed. Yet he and Martha had something endurable and fine. Their marriage would last forever. This little affair which temporarily filled him with delight would disappear and everything would be as it had been. He would be a man renewed, invigorated. Like a man coming back from a few weeks at a health farm. Elsa, who wore her inconstancy openly, would soon be looking for someone else. And Martha need never know.

She had called him a 'peach-picker' all the time before they were married and for some time after. It was her term of endearment. It put him in his place but at the same time showed a kind of pride in the fact that he had come so far from his tree, that he could read and write and had made it to university and had even crashed the barrier of the Chellow cul-de-sac.

She had never known that he was also a peach-planter. The tree he had accidentally planted had lived for twenty years on Chellow Street and for twenty years he had watched it grow like a sly father with a bastard child. Just how does a father watch over a bastard child, Mr. Ferrand? From a distance, madame. From a long way off.

At first he had only seen the tree on those days when the Murrays said to Martha, 'Come over for dinner and bring the children,' meaning, 'Leave that fellow you married behind in your suburban dwelling to perish of too much light, too many neighbours, suffocation of the mind.' Then for seven years after he and Martha had moved in to the Murray's house, he had been able to enjoy his tree in all its seasons; the blossoms in the springtime, the fruit, uncared for in the fall, dropping to the ground, wormy, uneatable. Once he had taken one of the fallen peaches home and cut off the good parts of it so that he could taste the fruit of his only tree. It had tasted like part of a wormy peach fit neither for jam nor "wine which never grew in the belly of the grape". (The English teacher had been a romantic but he had had the wrong book that year.)

His tree had been mashed down to make way for the Moxford's house, a poor replacement.

Through the kitchen window he saw dimly the stage set for his and Martha's wedding reception and even some of the ghostly actors. The garden then had been a gracious place which flourished under the attention of a full-time gardener. His own father, on that day, had inspected the shrubs and trees, bending down occasionally to hold some soil and let it sift through his fingers. It was not, in his view, a particularly good use of so much fertile land. His mother, regal in her long gown had sat enthroned beneath the willow mourning the loss of her second son, and told all who came near her that the wine was not a patch on the stuff her Yvan made at home from the local grape.

The picture faded slowly from his mind. One glorious day. Happy days. Happy years. Small children. 'Daddy, why does she call you a peach-picker?' 'Daddy when can we go to the farm again?'

He looked unwillingly again at the egg. Lying there in the cup, waiting to be put beside the bacon, it bothered him. Something he had been afraid to contemplate itched at his mind. Surely there would be some sign. In this he must be more ignorant than all the high schools in the neighbourhood. Elsa could not surely be totally irresponsible. He unzipped his fly and got the creature out to search for scars or what the textbook called lesions.

The front door opened and closed again. Hastily he straightened himself up. Martha was there! Solid and real.

She was wearing a dark red pantsuit of fine quality and endurable material.

"Hello dear. Have a good night?"

"Hectic. And you?"

Bob laughed as he poured coffee into two mugs and began to fry the egg.

"I don't think I can eat that this morning," she said. "Sit down and have your coffee and tell me what's in the newspaper."

He pulled the frying pan to one side and wondered who would eat the bacon and the still runny egg. "Somebody tried to push a Pakistani under a bus," he said as he sat down.

"Again. I suppose they'll charge a couple of kids."

"They have."

"They ought to be charging the parents, the teachers. All the comfortable, smug people who make slighting remarks. You know, the way I see it, it isn't the kid's hand doing the pushing, it's a hand on a long arm coming out of all the 'safe' middle-class places."

"It'll take time."

"Why do you have to get up so early. You look tired."

"I haven't been sleeping so well lately."

"I'll bring you some sleeping pills."

"Don't you dare."

"What!"

"I mean I don't like them. Not unless they're necessary."
Pills first. Then something in the soup. A little injection when the patient's back is turned. Dull the senses and turn the rampaging bull into a pussycat; make the lion able to lie down with the lamb and not touch it. Please. Not yet.

"What time did the kids come in?"

"Soon after you left."

"Did you talk to Dori?"

"She went straight to bed."

"It's time they were up."

"There's no school today. Remember."

12

Swift, sticky threads this small, dark Penelope used to bind him back into his place. Husband and father of children. Once even a churchgoer. Once a lover on bended knee who had promised eternal fidelity. Shit and shit. Time and again his mother had done the same thing. Arriving home in triumph or on the wave of some new discovery, he was brought down with, 'What have you done with your jacket?' or 'If you can't get home on time, you can't go out.' Never a suggestion, as in all the more recent books on child psychology, of giving the tardy child a watch.

"Isn't it time you were off?"

"I've a meeting at ten. There's no point in going down before."

"You could have waited in bed for me."

"Eh?"

She looked at him, hollow-eyed from being awake all night, and smiled, "You could have waited in bed for me."

She had come straight from having her hands in the blood of others and wanted now to touch him and stroke him and count his ribs and use words like scrotum and penis which destroyed him utterly. It had been quite all right when she was working at the clinic, referring the very ill to specialists and reassuring the merely worried. Since she had been overcome by the urge to go out and look after the accident victims in the emergency ward, she was, for him, surrounded by bloody images which he couldn't get out of his mind.

He fixed his gaze on the copper pans shining above the stove, every one of them an investment, every one of them heavy enough to be used as a lethal weapon. The little frilly drapes that covered the window matched the plastic benches either side of the small table.

She had picked up the dishcloth and squeezed it out and was wiping the counter very thoroughly. Was she about to lay him down and operate? Getting her table ready. A small but quick castration. Surreptitiously, he covered himself.

"We cleared up last night."

"I suppose we all get overcome by it at times."

"Mm?"

"The feeling that we have to work at our maximum usefulness. You know, like last year when you were already so busy and you went and headed up the M.S. appeal and made such a hash of it."

"It wasn't that bad."

"That's how I felt about being in Emergency. That I ought to be there. But I don't know . . . maybe I really belong to G.P. work. I'd be home at nights. We haven't had a night together, a proper one, for months."

"You'll have to take a lot of baths."

"What are you talking about?"

"That wasn't what I meant."

"Were you listening? I said I was thinking of changing jobs again."

"Martha, you're tired. Don't decide now. It must be exciting at the hospital. Voices calling you over the P.A. system. Legs to be set. Stitches. An appendix."

"For God's sake. You sound like a teenage kid. What's the matter with you. Anyway, my time's up on Friday. I'm probably not going back."

"This Friday?"

Once, when they were boys, he and his brother had been playing by the pond which was teeming with spring life. Several others had come to join them. They had firecrackers. The game was to catch a frog and stuff a firecracker in its mouth and light it. He had backed away quietly and hidden, out of sight, till the noise and the shrieking had stopped. Totally unheroic. Unable either to join in the game or to prevent what was happening. Unable to defend himself when THEY had found out and all hell broke loose. He had discovered the anguish of despising oneself. Like a bad taste once known, never forgotten, it had come back to him now.

With neither the honesty to leap up and shout, Martha, I've been deceiving you, nor to say to her firmly and decisively, Martha I have work to do, you go to bed; he sat there and said nothing.

"I'll take a couple of weeks off and then go back to the clinic. I've spoken to them and they were very pleased."

"You never mentioned it to me."

"What the hell has it to do with you? I thought you'd be pleased."

"I am pleased. Surprised."

"Let's go to bed then. You don't have to leave for an hour and the kids won't wake up. It looked to me when I came in as though you were about to masturbate into the frying pan."

"No," he squealed, startled at the strange sound. "No. I was just . . ."

"It's all right," she said in her I-am-a-doctor voice. "Let's go upstairs."

He walked up the stairs holding on to the handrail; the nice old wooden one had been replaced by wrought iron ten years ago because it was elegant. Small oil paintings of leafy greenery lined the route. The ceiling above them needed painting but this was not the moment for mentioning it and fetching out ladder and paints and brushes. A nice shade of pink would be right, some cherubs sculpted round the edge. They had, after all, been to Europe and knew a fine ceiling when they saw one. Seventeen steps there were, short and wide, made of fine old oak, polished but not slippery and all the time she had her hand on his gluteus medius.

"You undressed quickly," she said, as he sat there with the sheet drawn up to his chin, trying to infuse his mind with erotic images as she buttoned herself into a bright, white pyjama top, and put one knee on the edge of the bed and killed him dead.

At the end of the street, in the Quinn house with its ran-

15

dom eaves and tiled fantasies, Marianne Quinn sat on her half-moon desk listening to her own voice on the tape-recorder:

Mr. Ferrand is not yet my lover although I frequently walk past his house in shorts hoping that he will notice at least my ass. Middle-aged men who have lived and are living and have lined faces and secrets and the beginnings of a fear of death are much more interesting to me than young guys with shades of acne on their cheeks and big, damp hands and all their horrible lives before them.

I can't remember the first five years of my life although they tell me constantly that I should because they were happy and carefree. They draw me a picture of a golden park suspended in time, full of slow-moving swings that are totally safe, helterskelters with deep velvet mats at the end and nice, clawless pets.

Call-me-Henry, the analyst, complains that in every poem I write about sex. 'Find new subjects,' he says, as though they hang from the trees like sloths.

Yesterday Mrs. Crawley threw a plastic bag of milk at the milkman and screamed at him take that you bastard Peeping Tom.

Murder was committed less than an hour ago behind the Soper house.

I have begun to write a family chronicle which will run to three volumes and be full of truth and the voices of my parents.

This tape recorder is my notebook and soul and diary. This is not a multiple choice exam. All the questions must be answered. Mark the above statements out of ten for degrees of truthfulness.

Lilliane/Mother: who in those unremembered days had told her, 'Call me Lilliane, darling.' A vain young woman who tended the garden slightly, had servants, a man to do the heavy work, closets full of gossamer clothes and didn't want to be known as the mother of such an old, ungainly child.

Lilliane/Mother speaking: I discovered books again you see. I shudder and weep for all those wasted years. All that dreadful, artificial social life. You know the kind of thing. You give a cocktail party for thirty people and each of them gives one and before long your life is a dreadful circular carousel on which drinks are served. After all, when I was twenty-one, I had my M.A. in history. Classical languages were my second major. My ambition was to translate obscure documents. To spend my life in libraries. Dusty but so rewarding. Then I married Johnson and got caught up in his life. The parties we had then! For a while I read my French and Latin but soon there was no time. I think it was when I caught myself, for the seventeenth time in one day, smiling at somebody and saying, 'Lovely weather we're having, isn't it', and I realised that I had no other phrase to offer, nothing else to say, that I got off the carousel. I can do the *Review* crossword in a morning now and feel totally fulfilled. I have found my true self.

Lies all lies.

Father, in his study, would be studying precisely nothing. Wondering how soon his real day could begin and he could put his hand round a glass of whisky. On certain days, father the businessman picked up the briefcase containing the files with the gold G.Q. logo on them and went downtown, demeaning himself by talking to businessmen, discussing money, terms and quantities. He came home depressed, lay down for a while and then got up and went out again and stayed out till the phone rang, late, and Lilliane, dragging herself out of bed went to pick him up from whatever bar he was patronising that night, telling his 'I am Johnson Quinn' tale to a bleary-eyed barman who didn't give a shit.

Father speaking: Yes, we shared the same alma mater. He was at Oxford when I was there. Missed him at Yale by a year. Never misses a Christmas. Pile of cards signed, 'Yours, Wingy.' We called him Wingy in those days. If I wanted I could be in his cabinet tomorrow. Tomorrow. He always said to me, 'Quinny' — he called me Quinny — 'you can work for me any time.' I was there when he went to North Africa. I could have gone along. In the thick of the fighting his group were. I was on the dockside the day after they sailed. Missed them by a day. He'd asked for me specially. But there it was. So I went back to my desk. Shattering disappointment. But they told us we were heroes too. And I suppose we were. Those days were something. We were somebody. And when we went to the palace . . . Did I ever tell you about us being invited to the palace. . .

Lies all lies.

Marianne turned off her tape recorder. Day had begun. Very soon assorted strangers would come and beat on the door. In earlier, better times, a moat would have protected them, a moat full of angry crocodiles. And boiling oil, boiled fresh daily, would be poised on the turret roof to keep away Jehovah's Witnesses and Fuller brush men and unsuitable suitors.

Now only the giant elm stood guard over them. A monster tree, some of its branches dead, which had been allowed to grow too close to the tower window. Other trees round the house had been allowed to grow to mast-like heights, some had fallen and remained there, bent and uncut; and the conifers outside the front windows brushed the walls and reached the attic roof.

It might break down, the house so heavily designed by an architect who was a red-brick romantic and who must have worn knee-breeches and who rejoiced in building tower rooms for girls to let down their hair from the windows, to let up their lovers, to keep old ladies in, unsuitable and dirty old ladies.

Half a dozen houses had been built down each side of Chellow street twenty years after Gerald the Giant had built his minor palace on the imposing lot. He, ruthless and legendary great-grandfather, hadn't lived long enough to play squire to the intruders.

Marianne looked down at her notebook. She always wrote poetry between 6:30 and 8 a.m. stopping then to cast a curse on Dr. Ferrand who turned up around that time and did not know where her husband had spent part of the night.

"I would kill him," Marianne said aloud, "in many different ways."

"It's fashionable," her father had said, "to despise Tennyson." But still they had christened her Mariana. Later, when she had complained about it, they had referred her to the earlier poet and used him as their justification.

Softly she recited:

> Put your love away, love
> When the dawn frog croaks;
> Gold melts at the break of day, love,
> And everything's a hoax.

And then she cried because she hadn't written it herself. What could they expect from her when all the words that might have expressed her feelings had already been moulded into phrases and sold in small books under other names.

The analyst said she should write poetry to help sort herself out. Jack Grope (not his real name but his given name, given by her and always used by her), said the analyst had obviously told that to ninety per cent of all the young men and women in the country and that they were all out there now, hurrying to be first at the publishers with their slim and unattractive volumes; all of them cried alone at night; all of them watched beside windows. Jack Grope was a man of much body and surface mind but was not exactly into the deep pools of psychology. His creed was action now and then and all the time.

The long black car which parked occasionally in the early hours outside the Reverend Cline's was moving away. The orgy was over. The long howling scream had been brief. An exorcism? Julie and Anna, wild friends of Jack Grope, had gone in heavily for exorcism and said it was peculiar but more satisfying than plain ordinary sex. Perhaps in the back garden a virgin had been sacrificed, although the scream did seem to come from across the road. The men who got into the car and drove away were probably satanic priests and the Reverend Cline merely a servant, a tool of theirs.

Marianne had not told call-me-Henry about the Reverend Cline trying, on pretext of looking at her poetry, to fondle her and then drawing back as though it was not him but a ghost and then saying on his way downstairs, to her parents, that a visit to the Holy Land would be an educational delight and that she would be a welcome addition to his tour and might find in it a source of spiritual solace and comfort.

Comfort, Reverend Cline, is not having a strange hand shoved up your skirt. Mr. Ferrand's hand would be warm, and acceptable.

'My father's eyes are glassy now.' Not a great line. After she had read it aloud a few times, she crossed it out. At two o'clock they had tilted him out onto the doorstep. The taxi driver and Lilliane. Lilliane looking furtively around, sure that no one could see, thankful that Marianne and Granny were asleep in bed. Unaware that four eyes were watching. Granny, in the room above her, had been moving about then by her window.

> *"My father's eyes are like lobster flesh*
> *Streaked with red lines*
> *With as much understanding in them*
> *As the eye of a freshly caught, fairly intelligent lobster."*

She read it aloud. Better poems came like that. Quickly. On a sudden inspiration. Not too much alteration needed there. Laboriously she wrote it out with the broad-nibbed pen she used to produce her newly learnt Italic Script.

(At private school, wearing kilt and pin, they had taught her the use of the semi-colon and changed her name to Marianne.) Since she had stopped, to their momentary tight-lipped horror, going to university in the first year when she was doing so well in Art and History and French and Music — a nice civilising mixture of shit and ashes — they agreed, ah well, to let her spend some time at home. The money to be saved was not mentioned but did account in part for their acquiescence.

Ah well. She is an artist, a poet, a creative soul. And granny sighed upstairs unheard. Downstairs they said it could be understood. The family after all had come a long way from Gerald the Giant who in his early days had gone from store to store himself and had red hands from carrying suitcases in the winter. He would not have understood. The half-moon desk fitted so well at the turret window.

The Paper Boy had followed Mr. Ferrand up his driveway, had been following him closely all the way down the street on his early return home, and had thrown the paper on to his step, after him. A strange old man, he wandered about the houses as though he didn't already know them by heart. Because he wore kid's clothes and none of his customers looked closely at him, they never realised that he had been working the same route for forty years and knew every tiny detail of their lives.

She turned away from the window and glanced around her own room/womb. They had given her a quilted cover and hung above her bed the picture of a moated grange. The rest of the walls were covered with sheets of newspaper taped to the painted plaster underneath.

'Why not posters?' they had asked, thinking of brightly coloured paint and the normalcy of patterns.

'These are my posters,' she replied.

Perhaps today would be one of those days when the paper was so full of humanity crying out to be heard, vital tales of fighting and bombing and cruel deception that it earned the right to be glued over one of the others.

If you could learn about the truth, you could get a job, be a journalist, call-me-Henry had said. 'A catch-penny profession,' her father had pronounced it. Whatever that meant. 'Try it and see,' Jack Grope had suggested, unaware of the problem. But Jack Grope with his self-assured smell of leathery sweat had girls hanging off him everywhere and, with a lordly look, was always telling her to go and try something and see.

She turned on her tape recorder and began to speak aloud again. Click: Today my publisher is coming to lunch. There goes that untrue possessive again. He is a publisher. Not quite. He is an editor who works at the publishers which is owned in small part by a distant Quinn. Technically speaking, though, he can be called a publisher if not 'mine'. He is coming to see me. And my poems.

I sent him the Florida poems. They are about screwing on the beach under the stars like so many sea creatures come up out of the ocean to mate — almost like so many oyster-shells, two-halved and moving violently. And also the Panda poem, Panda, Panda, gleaming, bright. My parents think they are about flowers and nice scenery because I call them Pastoral Symphony. I'll read them aloud with the coffee.

Downstairs she could hear them moving about. Her mother would be in the kitchen, chopping up vegetables, stirring tomatoes into a sauce.

Marianne looked out at the Ferrand house. He was in there with her now. She had taken off her white coat and driven home. I think you should know, Dr. Ferrand, that your husband is sleeping with a night club singer and, by the way, have you looked in your daughter's bed lately? Going round the hospital with a lowered flashlight solicitously peering into bed after bed is very noble and nice. Try it at home sometimes, Dr. Ferrand. Take the dimmer off your flashlight. Two thirds of your patients are missing.

It was hard to imagine the good Dr. Ferrand herself having it off behind a hospital closet door with some green surgeon. 'Oh but I'm sterile.' 'Me too, who cares.' And a watching patient, creeping silently from the operating table which was now unsafe, coming to him and saying, 'By the way, Mr. Ferrand, I thought you should know.'

He was coming out of the house now, down the path to the street. Would he turn her way and float up to her window crying, 'Let me in, Marianne. I know you're there,' and make her the third woman he had laid in one night. He walked straight on towards the bus stop, determined, sober, knowing what he was doing. One of these days he would notice her and then the dreary night club singer and his tired old wife would never see him again.

Deciding to have a shower, she took off the clothes she had been wearing all night, flinging them at the newspapers on the walls, not caring that something went flying out on the breeze, through the screen-less window.

She turned back to her notebook. The lobster poem was not really that great. 'Dreame me some happinesse' had been written long ago. 'Dream me a lover' had been paraphrased in popular songs for centuries. There was not enough life in this room/womb. And what if, after lunch, the publisher said, 'These poems are just so many words, Marianne, and have no meaning at all.'

The milkbox was a natural dead-drop. And certainly the Paper Boy seemed to spend a lot of time lurking near the sides of these quiet old houses which had not, so far as Bob knew, done him any harm. On the pretext of looking for milk, Bob put his hand in the milkbox and found the blackmail note. Times of his defection noted. Price demanded.

"There's no milk," he said to Martha.

"There wouldn't be. I didn't order any today," she replied.

Bob put the note into his pocket and went out of the front door as though this was an ordinary, normal kind of day. AND WHAT ABOUT YOUR WIFE, MR. FERRAND? Ah. Yes. Well. I tried, didn't I? My mother was often surrounded by steam. YOUR WIFE IS A LADY, A DOCTOR. What if she was standing at the window, now, watching him.

He turned back to look but the Chellow Street windows were secretive and dark. She could be standing there naked and no one would be able to see her from the street.

Martha was standing there. She was watching him walk reluctantly down the road as though he didn't want to go to work, backing up, going forward again, turning almost completely round.

She wondered whether he realised how lucky he was that at his age he hadn't so far felt twinges of arthritis or nagging stomach pains and that only certain mental abnormalities betrayed his age. She wished, as she watched him, that just one time she had been able to persuade him to buy one suit of a decent quality. What was he thinking now as he walked along? Left alone at night was he feeding on fantasies, satisfying himself with girlie magazines and leaving no place for her? He never wore the Cardin ties she bought him every Christmas. Was he, like the clichéd doctors' children, feeling deprived of the attention she gave to others and fretting that there was not enough for him?

She could tell that at the moment his own work was depressing him. He was the only person she had ever known who took a cottage cheese sandwich to lunch, soggy and damp because of the pineapple he added to it: it had to be carefully wrapped in a wetproof bag. The delays in building, the constant hassle with the environmentalists, 'What do they think we are, monsters?', the fear that from now till retirement there would be no more worthwhile projects. All of it could make a man feel inadequate, impotent, and cause him to build an unreal, imaginary life and to make an enemy out of a harmless paper boy. As she watched him, he sidestepped in and out of the gutter and waved his arms. She sighed.

BOB WAS BACKING DOWN THE ROAD SURROUNDED BY REPORTERS WHO WERE DANCING AT HIM LIKE SHADOW BOXERS HOLDING OUT MICROPHONES. CAMERAS WERE DOLLYING TO AND

— Just a word, sir. Now that you've been elected to this high office, have you a message for the people?

— It is important to recognise that this has not happened overnight. Nor is it limited to this small area. Rather, what we have seen over the past years has been a natural disintegration. Natural, given this set of circumstances, this place, these people and the fact that we always consult the committee of the local Humane Society.

— Could you tell us what you intend to do about the post office and the infamous ringer system, sir?

— That hardly falls in my bailiwick as Energy Csar, does it? But I can tell this, that I shall not rest until the people in charge are made aware that mailmen are indeed farming out their routes to these crooks who are making a good thing of stealing from milkboxes, taking parcels left by other delivery men and I may say of — blackmail!

— Will you be making any great changes locally, sir?

— Certainly. I am thinking of running a North-South railway right through the middle of this area. About where we're standing. Great, clanking iron trains coming from, say, Barrie, straight through to downtown.

— Has any member of your family ever been elected to anything before?

— My father was once president of the Lions in Lincoln County. They sold lightbulbs for charity.

— So they must be very proud of you back home. Being elected Screw of Chellow Street.

— It goes without saying.

Bob walked on with the questions still echoing round him. And what brought you to this area in the first place? Why don't you drive the LTD to work? Why don't you wear the Cardin ties your wife buys you each Christmas? We don't like your Québecois name or your night habits. When you screw around why don't you go further afield like the rest of us do?

TIME, MR. FERRAND, I'M FROM TIME. OUR READERS WOULD
LIKE TO KNOW THE FACTS AND FIGURES OF YOUR LIFE.

In the beginning there were diapers and humidifiers
which turned into damp affection and then condensed into
tears. Simply, simplistically, your word I believe, it was something like that. There was this warm flesh which united us
once and which was not advertised as perishable. AND ECO-
NOMICALLY SPEAKING? Time now to dump the black-edged
insecurities.

Instead of walking down the road on their side as he nor-
mally did, Bob had crossed the road on purpose, it seemed, to
peer into the Sopers' driveway. Had he been hoping for a
glimpse of Alva? Was Alva watching him too? If Harris spent
less time in his laboratory over the garage perfecting his nasty
little electronic devices and more time with his wives, there
might be less of a turnover. Though there was more there, perhaps, than met the eye.

Alva, who was never seen before noon, had come furtively into the Emergency Department a few weeks ago at a
cold, early hour to be treated for burn marks in an unusual
place. 'Promise you won't tell, Dr. Ferrand.' And Dr. Ferrand
had instinctively put two fingers to the side of her head and
given a brownie promise that was even now more binding
than the Hippocratic oath.

Because she was a doctor they expected answers, unbro-
ken promises, advice and a total self-sufficiency on her part.
Even Cline, next door, the chaplain of Chellow Street, the
urbane cleric, had come to her once about his wife. And she
had not said to him, 'Behind every alcoholic there is a reason.
Is it you, Reverend Cline? Think about it.' She had given him
sympathy and lemonade and he had tried to persuade Dori
into baby-sitting his wife's precious cat. An instinct had made
Dori say no, sharply, and the Reverend gentleman had turned
away from the child's glare.

Martha knew that Bob loved his children. True, a wall seemed to have grown up between them and him. A solid wall of politeness and platitudes and unsynchronised times. But there could have been the rest of his life to take the wall down again. Why was she dismissing him into a past conditional?

The Reverend Cline was out there now planting a rose tree he had moved from round the back. An unlikely time for a keen gardener to move his favourite plants.

Parallel to the Moxfords, Bob had hesitated again. Martha laughed to herself. He couldn't be looking up to see HER. No one could take La Moxford seriously. She and her sinister husband had insulted the street by moving into it. They had assaulted the street with their unpleasant habits: hers of lying outside in their strip of backyard wearing a tiny string bikini and playing loud music which curdled the mind; his of shouting loudly to her as she lay there from one of their top slit windows. But they had progressed from being a topic of indignant discussion to being a pair of cartoon characters. A swatch of blonde hair, a large red mouth, the stole: her. Slick black hair, small eyes, large hands: him. They rated now no more than a shrug, a smirk, a lifting of outraged but amused hands.

As he waited for the bus, Bob looked back at the Moxfords'. She was in there now lying on that furry stole, the hairs caressing her body as she recited a litany of men's names. Was one of them ever his? Did she look out of the long window and sigh for him as he went by, seeing his half-bald head as sexy, his plain white shirts a sign of steady and admirable conservatism?

Martha felt her own body under the housecoat. Compared to Alva Soper she might have been a boy. Lately she had taken to walking past mirrors with her head averted. Modern makeup could do wonders. The advertisements all said so. But she had no faith in cream and coloured paste. She opened the door and looked out and could still see Bob there, at the bus stop, waiting, far down the street, in a group of late leavers. He would be the last to get on.

"I've always given the right damn answers," she said aloud to no one in particular.

Letting his eyes travel up and down the whole cul-de-sac, Bob shook his head. It was not surprising that the Paper Boy and his accomplices wanted to cut at the roots of this whole area. What was good in it? What had ever been good about barriers? But the Paper Boy's methods were wrong, and two wrongs. . . .

Yes indeed, there had been a time, years ago, when she had watched him each morning as he left for work. But as he looked back, the window of their house was a distant, dark, unseeing eye. From the tower window of the Quinn place, a piece of light material seemed to be fluttering like a flag. Panties? A bra? Was sex dimming his vision?

THE BUS IS COMING, THE BUS IS COMING. MR. FERRAND, NEWLY-ELECTED SCREW OF CHELLOW STREET, MUST GO TO HIS OFFICE. EAT YOUR HEARTS OUT, WOMEN!

The bus came and swallowed Bob and the others whole and carried them away.

Part Two

Bob rustled the piece of paper in his pocket hoping one time to put his hand there and find it gone. Anonymous notes must be destroyed. Threats should be ignored. A clear conscience is like a shining sword — and damn rare. Let the animal who wrote the thing do his worst. Let him speak out. There was only one thing to do and that was to meet the whole thing head on. Later, when the fighting and the shouting had died and the horses had ridden off and the trumpet had sounded its last note, and the crumbling ruins of his former life were smoking like a razed city, he would pick up the pieces that were left. No family. No wife. No home. Sitting on a step on Jarvis Street, wearing a good suit three sizes too large, a charity suit donated by the widow of a rich but dead tycoon of whom no ill was spoken but plenty thought, he would wait for somebody to give him a dollar towards a bottle of St. Emilion, grateful that the sun was shining.

'I don't think we can progress any further in the present climate of opinion.'

Cold winds veering eastwards, icy blasts coming in from the South and the precipitation advancing from the general direction of Montreal does not happen to be money.

'These delays are putting the whole industry at risk, Mr. Chairman.'

'How long before we're actually closing places down. No heat.'

'That kind of hysterical thinking leads to panic.'

'As you all know,' the Chairman said, 'we have to have our findings in by next month and I think it's important now that we come to a definite decision on the colour of the binding.'

'Christ!'

'We're talking of several thousand copies. University libraries. Things like that. Red is cheaper.'

'Leather? Cloth?'

'Best quality worm-proof vinyl.'

Delaying his return to the office a little longer, delaying in fact his conversation with Mercer about the meeting, Bob went into the men's wear shop on the corner. Banners across the window proclaimed a twenty-per-cent-off-everything sale. Inside, a carnival atmosphere had been created by draping streamers across the ceiling and by decorating the walls with a collection of Edwardian hats. Each salesman was wearing a carnation in his buttonhole. The striped shirts, of a well-known and reputable make, lay in an enticing heap on a table in the centre of the store.

"These shirts haven't been marked down yet," Bob said to the assistant. Wanting to say to him, 'Look, I've been coming here for twenty years. I bought my first decent shirt here. Can't you show me some enthusiasm, a little nice welcome, brush the dust out of the way when I walk in?' But a city doesn't remain a village.

"That is the sale price, sir."

"They were this price two weeks ago."

"Two weeks ago. Well that's it, isn't it." The man had a bristly, brush-down moustache and a grim certainty in his own logic. "I mean in two weeks, the cost of them has gone up twenty percent. Labor, Material. All pushes the prices up. That is a bargain price now, sir."

The awful re-heated egg had now churned itself into a cloggy mass in Bob's stomach. "Liars and thieves. It's people like you who push the prices up and create inflation. Look how this lousy shirt's made."

Tearing and ripping, he pulled the shirt out of its package and tugged at the sleeve. When the assistant tried to wrest it from him, it came apart like a wishbone. Leaving the assistant gaping at the rag in his hand, Bob took several more shirts out of their bags and strewed them round the floor.

"That's what I think of your phony sale," he shouted. "Call the police. Let's have this written up in the paper. I've been buying shirts here for twenty years. And you'll never see me again."

He strode out of the store and went across the road towards the office. He leaned up against the wall to get his breath back and to let the egg lie down again and to wonder why there were tears in his eyes. The faces that came towards him were stony, ungiving; a blend of oriental, caucasian, green Martian, darkest black. He was an outsider now in what had once been his city.

A shaggy youth with a beatific expression on his face, sandwiched between two boards which proclaimed the Coming of the Kingdom, drifted lightly towards him, thrust a lollipop in his face and murmured, "Suck this for peace."

Action equals therapy.

They should all be sued for invasion of privacy, all these itinerant loafers who offered pamphlets and flags, and the bald-headed buggers who gave out nail-hard cookies in the streets. In Russia they would have been carted away and sent slowly to Siberia to hack out a living in the frozen tundra. As he looked back over his shoulder he saw with satisfaction that the bringer of peace was holding his ankle, glaring at him belligerently and making unpleasant gestures with the lollipop.

The office building was in front of him. Man had gleefully created these giant space-saving skyscrapers, rejoicing in the shape of new outlines. A city must, in silhouette, look like a set of toy blocks randomly placed. And then, malevolently, these same buildings had leaned towards each other to dwarf and terrify their creators, shutting out the sky.

The Manley building: a shoe box that some child had divided into compartments and filled with desks and filing cabinets to scale, and cut-out men and women. It was a shoe box among shoe boxes. A man might spend a day in the wrong one and not be noticed. But teacher was ringing the bell. Mother was shouting 'Time to come in,' and he and Jimmy were running towards the farmhouse door with Ginger close behind them.

He climbed the stairs because it was only four flights and good for the heart like sex and some wine and bran and egg-less days.

Mercer was sitting at his desk talking into the phone, "Je veux parler à Monsieur Smith, s'il vous plaît. Smith. Ah merci. Hm. Some kind of frog day off," he explained, replacing the receiver. His head, when he leaned back was framed by pictures of reactor vessels, sites, tubes and various well-signed certificates. "Day off!" he said. "More likely they're all getting ready to move in here. What are THEY trying to do? Ruin the whole country? The Prime Minister's gone off his head again. Don't tell me what went on at your meeting. That fool Everett said it all depends on the hearings, right?"

"More or less. All bound in red worm-proof vinyl."

"I sometimes think the only people in this whole world with any sense are the Israelis. They want something. They go get it. Look at that affair in Uganda."

For a moment they both sat there, lost in a small dream of adventure, of creeping up on an unsuspecting enemy, of camouflage and webbed hats, of the quick effective strike, a few casualties, a few dead, including one of theirs; well that was the price one paid. That was the risk, the adventure. That was life. Life in the picture of a hard, smiling man leaning against a plane with the wind blowing through his hair.

"Maybe we should offer Idi Amin a nuclear power station."

Something new and terrible out of Africa. Deep, dark things were happening on mysterious continents and glib but totally uncomprehending politicians made answers that drove the wise men in their backrooms to despair. Powermongers were hawking their wares and arms vendors were counting money, and here in this small office, a certain Bob Ferrand, of no significance whatever, brought out from his pocket a poor-looking piece of paper on which was written, 'Tues. 5.43 Thurs. 5.39   Sat. 5.17 $15.99'.

"I'm not sure whether to take it seriously. It could be a joke. A mistake. But the times are right," he said when he handed the note to Mercer and explained it to him.

Mercer had long since perfected the art of using the office swivel chair correctly. He turned away from the desk now and held the note up. Then he turned back and tapped his fingers on the arm of the chair but said nothing.

Fifty if a day, Mercer was. The skin on the back of his hands was beginning to show his age. They had worked together for fifteen years, ten of them a time of prosperity in their industry which had made the relationship easy. In all that time they had rarely spoken of personal matters. Like boys poring over a railway set, they had closed out the other world. Yet now, Bob wanted to say to Mercer, 'Who are you? Are you all right? Am I going to be all right? Shall I come through this? Why is there no one to ask but you? A man should have friends.' Once when Bob had begun to talk about his family, Mercer had cut him short with an offhand reference to 'the place where you live' as though there was a wall of expensive real estate between them.

"I need some advice," Bob said. "I don't want Martha to know. And there's the kids."

"Eh?" Mercer asked.

"This blackmail note. I think it's the Paper Boy."

"A blackmail note. If I got one of these Hilda wouldn't believe it. She'd laugh. You've seen Hilda?"

Bob had once seen a lady being hurried down the stairs by Mercer. A large woman who looked like a prize fighter manqué. He nodded.

"I suppose people wonder why I married her. I don't think I did. We used to go to the movies a lot in those days, when I was a student, in a group, you know. Gradually all the others left or got married. There was only me and Hilda alone in the back row. They were horror movies mostly. I held her hand. Her knee. Just for reassurance. To know that someone was there. Suddenly I was at this wedding. Rings. Ribbons. Cake. People singing. I never remember proposing. Even now anybody bangs a fork on a plate, by accident, in a restaurant, I go through the roof. I still watch horror movies. I don't know that I want to hear about your wife, your kids. My daughter takes after Hilda and my son meditates. God knows what about."

"I'm sorry."

"Her face sets sometimes in lines. Her mouth's like a kind of trap. . . ."

"I'd like some advice."

"Ever since my wedding day, I've never dared give anybody advice. Where that side of life's concerned, I'm an illiterate."

"The note. The blackmail. It's a kind of business proposition."

"And sometimes — at night — she makes me sleep in the same room as her or what would the neighbours think. Oh God what do they think! So I walk down the street in the mornings, briskly, as though I've just spent the night with Brigitte Bardot although it's far more likely it was the Vampire's Daughter or the Blue Monster from the Unutterable Depth."

"I could lie in wait, you see. Have done in fact."

Suddenly business-like, Mercer picked up his phone and snapped, "Hold all my calls." Then he said to Bob, "Fifteen ninety-nine. How goddam cunning!"

"Cunning?"

"I can see you wouldn't want Martha to know."

But who knew what Martha knew? She had inside her head all the pages of great books of anatomy and specifics. She had seen and touched more people than he would ever say hello to in his life. And she could, and maybe should, have been a well travelled woman with an album of chic photographs of herself, on and off skis, with her arms round people called Ercole and Jeanne and Siggy. She knew perhaps that all she had got as a reward for her hard work was an unfaithful husband and was, even now, brewing hemlock and preparing to lay charges.

"Is it over then?" Mercer asked.

"What?"

"Your affair?"

"Ah." Bob had never thought of dignifying his sexual excursion by that name. But that is what it would be called. An 'affair'. He was having an 'affair' with a nightclub singer who belted out primitive jungly songs that stirred black magic in the body. "It's great at the moment. But she's not exactly. I mean it could — be over any time."

"A good lay is she?"

"Well — yes."

"If it was over you could tell the guy to stuff his notes."

"He could still tell Martha."

"That's O.K. when it's over. You can tell her yourself. Have a great reconciliation scene."

"You watch too many late movies, Mercer. It wouldn't work out that way. This could ruin my life."

"I'd still fight it," Mercer said as he pressed the button down. The phone began to ring. There was work to do.

As Bob went to his own office, he felt nothing like a crusader. Into other men's lives came great, challenging holocausts, vulpine adversaries, dark, passionate women. Other men's private wars were fought in dry deserts and deadly arctic wastes. Into his own life, a measure of it perhaps, had fluttered this lousy piece of paper. On account of it, he had to gird himself, put on the favours of one of his ladies, and go out to fight.

"Oh there you are, Mr. Ferrand," Margie said. "Your wife's called twice. She's quite hysterical."

"What does the old man want all this stuff for?"

"Some anonymous weirdo keeps sending him notes about a conspiracy on Chellow Street."

"Anonymous notes are supposed to be for burning."

"It might be the Mayor."

"What am I going to do then, loiter about?"

"If you can't think of anything else, go see the Quinns."

'In their gracious home on the Chellow cul-de-sac Johnson Quinn lives with his family in a delightful Renaissance style. Each member of the family pursues his own intellectual hobby and they meet at mealtimes for a stimulating exchange of ideas and the kind of conversation which has almost gone out of style.

Mrs. Quinn, who gave up a hectic social life some years ago in order to pursue Truth in Literature, is, she feels, making a much greater contribution to life in Canada.

When his business affairs allow him time, Mr. Quinn studies oriental philosophy. His main interest lies in Buddhism and the development of the soul.

Mrs. Quinn-Burden, surviving child of Gerald (the Giant) Quinn, makes up stories in her spare time and hopes one day to find a ghost writer. She has, she said when spoken to briefly in the hallway, a story to tell which would pin back the ears on a donkey. Time has not altered her strong Quinn character.

Marianne, only child of the Johnson Quinns, is living at home and writing poetry. Chellow Street, she says, is a very interesting place to live.'

"What's this crap?"

"You said to visit the Quinns."

"Did I? This is a newspaper for Christ's sake, not a daily edition of tales from a sunshine town."

'Mr. and Mrs. Johnson Quinn who live in their fine gracious home on Chellow Street manage to combine a variety of intellectual pursuits with their social and business obligations. The Library of their house testifies to the fact that reading is not out of fashion here. Marianne Quinn, their only child, expects to have her first volume of poetry published before long. Mr. Quinn's mother, Mrs. Quinn-Burden, takes a great interest in the garden and also writes fiction.'

"What's this crap?"
"The Quinn piece. I condensed it. Like you said."
"It's too goddam long and you haven't mentioned Gerald."

'Mr. and Mrs. Johnson Quinn, living in the house which Gerald (the Giant) Quinn built on Chellow Street, with his mother, a keen gardener, and their daughter, Marianne, a free-lance journalist, are planning to give a garden party before long.'
"Are they?"
"She said something about it would be nice. Like old times."
"It'll do for the social page."

This is my mother — do sit down — over here you get a view of the garden — dry — sweet sherry is for barbarians — excuse my husband — not on that chair if you don't mind — this is my mother, hush mother — we often listen to *Lakmé* at lunch — is that glass clean — do you believe in the soul — what would have happened if she had lived — my wife's pre-occupation — it's a long time since we've been to Europe — publishing in this country — I mean of course Vir-gin-ia — immigrants with weird names — did she have to put those pebbles in her pocket — do nothing for business — if she had lived to be seventy, say — hush mother — here comes our little girl now.

Feeling as though he had been come at by three sharp-eyed parrots in a smelly cage, Jim Gordon turned as a young woman with gorgon hair and no apparent physical handicaps entered the room. Like Undine breasting the waves, she waded through aromatic layers of stale cabbage water, old, damp house, neglected human skin, and reached down to unplug the record player so that *Lakmé* died on a screech and a scrape. Helping herself to a glass of sherry, she turned to him, her left nipple thrusting through the strange knotted-string dress she was wearing, and said, "Good morning."

String. It was made of string. Knotted. The knots not close together. Go and see her, the Great All-Canadian Publisher had said. Who knows. She's a Quinn. She says she's handicapped. Confined. Sexual Yearnings from a Wheelchair. Picture on the front. Coast to coast promotion. Go see what else she's got. He raised his glass to her and murmured, "You're not a cripple."

She only had time to smile at him before the parrots' chorus started up again.

"Marianne isn't the only writer in the family."

"What do you honestly think about the state of publishing in this country? A lot of goddam untalented foreigners get into print just because their names are Horvekci or Karamavicz."

"Tell me though, what effect it might have had if she'd lived to be seventy or so. What else might she not have written?"

"So much pissy poetry. So many half-assed novels."

"I should imagine . . ."

"I've sent my manuscript to every publisher in the country. It always comes back without even a note. I mean to illustrate it with dried wild flowers, rock columbine, Indian turnip, wood anemone."

An even stranger smell rose above the others.

"Oh my God. The celery casserole."

So she was sitting next to him now at the dining room table, a massive hunk of oak hewn by Gerald himself. She was sitting next to the man who had read her poems. Let them talk. Let the strange eyes on the wall opposite glare down. Later he would tell her. Even now, before they had spoken to one another, he was holding open, just for her, the door into another world.

The silver on the sideboard looked sadly black and the days when the chandelier's prisms had seen soap and water every Wednesday were long gone. Surreptitiously Gordon wiped his fork on his sleeve.

Photographs lined the dim, panelled walls; portraits of Quinns and their partners and children; and one engraving of an Imperial Ball which Gerald had attended during an ill-timed business trip to Russia in 1917. A bomb had exploded on the ballroom floor and singed his wife's expensive gown, confirming Gerald's views that Capitalism was Right and Good. For the rest of his life he wondered, aloud, at its over-throw on the great Russian continent where, peasants aside, there had been quite a few intelligent people.

Gerald agreed with those who saw the revolution as a series of errors compounded by Oblomovism. He was sure that It could not happen Here and would not have happened There if several events, occurring in unlucky conjunction, had not made it do so.

'They met Lenin by mistake. All those people were there because they were expecting a troop train. A train full of wounded relatives from the front. They were excited, looking forward to having Vladimir and Ivan and Dmitri back on the stove top. Nearly the whole population of St. Petersburg was there. Of course they cheered when the train pulled into Fin-land station. Of course they fell silent when all that got out was this weedy guy in the brand new worker's cap that he'd bought two stops back. Of course they stood still and listened to him; they wanted to know when the troop train was coming. Of course they cheered when he spoke. He'd been away so long, he had this funny accent and they thought he was telling them that Vladimir and Ivan and Dmitri were just a few miles back down the track and would be right along, in the new dawn.

That's the true story of Lenin coming to St. Petersburg. I know. I was there. The rest is history.'

Thus had spoken 'The Giant', founder of these family fortunes, who looked down at them now from his gilt oval frame. Eyes a little close. Nose a little hooked. Lips a little tight.

"My father," Granny said, speaking for the first time, nodding at the portrait.

"Hush Granny," Lilliane said automatically, making gestures to Marianne about her disarray. Marianne neatly pushed the nipple back into its fragile cover with the end of her spoon.

"Celery casserole," Johnson said. "My wife has quite a way with celery."

"Have a roll, Mr. Gordon. I make them myself with bran and wheat germ and dulse."

"Thank you. I rarely eat much lunch."

"So I wrote a book myself. Before I got interested in Buddhism. All about war at sea and a giant whale and a whore who'd been in the whale's belly for three years and suddenly got thrown out among all these horny sailors. Never bothered to send it out. Nobody's interested in reality. I read it myself now and then. Nine hundred and three pages. Always enjoy it."

"Perhaps Mr. Gordon might look at it, Johnson."

"Ah. Well. We don't. . . ."

"And besides," Johnson went on, "your business is riddled with fags."

Lilliane's trailing mauve sleeve drooped into the casserole dish as she thrust the rolls at him. Her short, badly cut hair stuck out like overbleached straws. Lines round her eyes crisscrossed in a fascinating railway yard pattern. Wistfully she murmured to no one in particular, "There were a lot of parties in those days."

"I don't think he wants to know that, mother," Marianne said.

"But that was before. Before we decided to live a different kind of life. We thought of it first you know. The Importance of Finding Oneself. Being Aware. All those things. It's become so fashionable now as to be ridiculous. Don't you find that what is fashionable soon becomes ridiculous, Mr. Gordon?"

"Don't ask him dumb questions, Lilliane."

"Coffee for everyone?" Marianne asked.

"Let's have it in the drawing room, dear. You know. The silver tray. The heirloom cups."

"A publisher eh?" Granny glared across at him, her eyes a copy of those on the wall behind her and all the others round the table. The parrots turned instantly into basilisks.

"I have a story," Granny went on. "I've gone over and over it in my head. It only needs to be written down."

"Hush granny."

"It'll have to be illustrated. A picture of a man with a spade. Rocks. No blood though. Hardly any blood. Some people have a lot more blood than others. I don't have much. I eat a lot of cookies and the crumbs soak it up. He had none."

"My mother hallucinates."

"I do not."

"It's time for your rest mother."

"I have a lot of rests. I'm never tired."

Lilliane and Johnson quickly surrounded the old lady and led her off towards the stairway.

"Look at the books in the library, Mr. Gordon. Some fine first editions."

"You can dance for us tonight, mother."

"I'll get out your gypsy skirt and tambourine."

"We'll get the music ready and before dinner you can dance for us."

The parrots went on up into the roof somewhere and he could no longer hear their voices. Jim Gordon slipped quietly into the drawing room and sank down into a large dusty chair. Maybe it would take them a long time to throw a black cloth over the old lady's cage. Maybe he could sue the Great All-Canadian Publisher for assault on the spirit.

Marianne came into the room with four mugs hooked round the fingers of one hand and a coffee pot in the other. She set them all down on the table and came towards him, both nipples showing. Now she was approaching her judge, her maker or unmaker, her line to life. "What do you think of my poems, Mr. Gordon?"

"Why did you say you were crippled from birth? I was expecting a wheelchair."

"You've come, haven't you?"

"There are other ways."

"What about the poems."

"The poems. Yes. We like them, Marianne. We like the way you use words. And the feeling behind them — obviously — er — deeply felt. And if you keep on? . . . But we also feel you need to see a bit more of life. There's a world out there."

"I haven't any money."

Was she going to cry? God! And no place to conceal hanky or kleenex. How could he wipe her eyes without touching her breasts.

"You could earn some. It would be a good way to see — life."

"I'm not trained for anything."

No one in thirteen years of school had taught her how to wait on people in a store. They paid so much an hour which added up in five days a week but did one want to sell one's time so cheap? Washing hair in beauty salons would mean running her fingers all day through other people's scalps and letting water drip down their faces till they groped for a towel and cried out as the cold changed too quickly to hot. Kentucky fried chicken cried out for help to come and roll legs and breasts in breadcrumbs there under the striped awning, and sell it to all kinds of people who were demanding and relentless. Modelling was only for people with straight up and down legs and hands that hung nicely over the arms of chairs.

"I'd thought of journalism," she said.

"It's a good profession. But do you know what it means to be a beginning reporter?" She was kneeling in front of him, looking into his face while the temptation to put his fingers through the holes in her dress became intense. "It means going out to meetings, fires, courtrooms, social gatherings. Making sure you spell the names right."

"And facts."

"The facts have to be right too."

"What else could I do?"

"If you found something in the city, so you could live at home, here in this cage, sorry, you could earn quite a bit, they wouldn't ask you for board, surely, you have a beautiful body."

"To earn money with?"

"Mmm? Sorry. I'm a bit distraught."

Johnson and Lilliane came into the room and sat down close to him while Marianne poured the coffee. Before they could resume their parrot dialogue, the girl, the nearly naked, uncrippled girl, brought out her poems and sat down on a low stool and began to read aloud.

> *The sea-backed monster on the sand*
> *Makes rhythmic love;*
> *Lovers in shells with fluted edges*
> *Strike out one of the above . . .*

Gordon moaned in various kinds of pain and hoped no one noticed.

"I think she's talking about oysters," Johnson muttered and closed his eyes.

"Why did she go?" Martha looked at him with the ravaged face of all the mothers in the world and he had no answers for her because he wasn't of the tribe and didn't know the language. Until now Martha had been the central, fragile axis of a sphere which someone had kicked, tilting it, making her kitchen shelves slope inwards so that at any moment all the jars and plates and packages might fall into the middle of the floor.

Dori had gone. She had left in the night while he was out. Had she perhaps come to look for him and found the bed not slept in? He tried hard to retrieve some memory, a feeling of what he had thought at that age. But there only returned to him an echo of days when his arms and shoulders ached from hours spent in the sun picking peaches, sorting them, packing them. It remained as a taste of peach jam and peach pie and wasps, and a hangover from a stolen jug of wine. Of thoughts there remained not one. Of feelings there was only a glimmer of dim resentment whose object he could not recall.

It was too late now to plant peach trees as a hedge against (the trouble with young people nowadays is that they haven't enough to do) his children's future. The orchard would not grow quickly enough. And, in any case, the peaches might well be left to rot on the trees when the kids had worked out the cost-benefit analysis.

"She'll come back," he said. "Kids at this age do this kind of thing. She's showing us she's an individual."

"But what did she mean," Martha went on, "in her note, about us leading an irregular life. We both go out to work. But so do a lot of other parents. Our lives are simple."

YES INDEED. WE PAY OUR BILLS AND EAT THREE MEALS A DAY

46

AND ARE NOT OUTRAGEOUS IN OUR APPEARANCE AND RARELY MISS
A SYMPHONY CONCERT AND KEEP TIME WITH THE REST OF THE
WORLD AND OUR NON-EXISTENT DOG DOESN'T SOIL THE SIDEWALK.

" 'Irregular' ", she repeated. "I asked Sam what she
meant, whether he thought our lives were 'irregular', and he
said to ask you."

"What in hell did he mean by that!"

"Bob, why are you so angry?"

"I am not angry," he shouted.

Angry! What a feeble word. He felt like going out to the
highest point in the city and letting out a primeval bellow,
beating his chest and yelling, 'Why me?' But he was afraid of
the answer and of the Paper Boy calling up the truth to him.

All around him, in all the large and small streets of the
city, people were committing sins of the flesh and the spirit in
confident abandon and they were left alone to lead lives of
unbounded joy. Why had he, Robert Ferrand, been selected
to suffer? Somewhere back in his university days, they had
missed out a vital course. He had not been forewarned of this,
or given answers to repeat to this woman who was sitting
opposite him demanding why her daughter had left while
grass cuttings dripped off his shoes on to the kitchen floor.
And she had the right to an answer.

From the top of the same tower, he wanted to yell out,
'Rejected. I am rejected.' His erstwhile mistress, lovely soft
word that it was, had phoned him at home, probably to cancel
their appointment. His daughter whom he had cherished and
nourished and for whom he had bought at least a dozen silver
charms and whose night-time fears he had soothed away
(excepting only this one last time) had turned away from him.
Sam was a distant relative. Only Martha with her sharp knife
and her white coat and a similar jagged tear in her soul was
left.

"I've always kept the grass cut," he said.

"I wonder what I did wrong," was Martha's reply.

At such moments did men murder their wives. Oh sure

they killed them too in times of heated passion. At moments of discovery (you are surprised — I am astounded), and in the steamy hot weather downtown when there's no escape from the heat in the streets and liquor burns in the mind, they kill. But also in cool and pleasant rooms where everything is covered in soothing pale green cloth and paint, when a man knows he is as guilty as hell and she turns to him and says, 'What have I done wrong?', then too a man reaches for a handy weapon and ends it all quickly.

Bob took hold of Martha's neat hand, turning it over to see whether there was blood crusted under the fingernails. She wore only her wedding ring; the small diamond ring, bought with help from his father and several bushels of peaches, was kept in its box and worn only after working hours. A fragile-looking hand which was marked now by brown spots and was also a weapon, a tool of the trade, indispensable.

"And to go to the Weibs," she cried, and finally put her head on his shoulder and sobbed. For a moment he wanted to press her hands on to her face and let her own tears wash them clean. Nothing was more cleansing than fresh salt tears. Any ancient Greek knew that.

"I'm sorry," she mumbled.

"It's better than Comet," he replied.

"I don't always understand you any more."

He dabbed at her eyes with his hankie. It was a darkish colour. The city was a dirty place and he often wiped his hands on his hankie and forgot to get a clean one. Her face was lightly streaked with greyish smudges. And as he returned the hankie to his pocket he felt the note again, the blackmail note he had found in the milkbox. And he could say to her now, 'And by the way dear, the other night on my way back from a meeting, I stopped in at the Blue Knight for a beer and guess what?' Or he could say, 'Let's air all our problems at once dear.' Or, 'We're adults, you and I. . . .'

"I'll make you some tea," he said. "Go and sit in the living room. Try and relax."

She sat in the living room surrounded by happy, chatter-
ing young girls who were assured in their attitudes, well-
dressed and fresh-complexioned. They were not Dori's friends
who might have been here yesterday. They were the shades of
the friends of Martha Murray whom they had just voted most
attractive, most popular, most likely to succeed. They had
believed, those girls, in God, in their own mighty fathers, in
the power of money, that conservatism was Right and that
their own health and good looks and youth would last for ever
and ever. She kept in touch with a few of them. Some had
been dismayed by her aberrant marriage. A few had successful
careers. Others had brought up fine-looking well-mannered
daughters and sons. But she could not judge them, ever again;
she had crossed the line, moved to the other side, joined the
ranks of the failed mothers, those whose children left home. I
HAVE NO DEFENCE, YOUR HONOUR. I THOUGHT I WAS DOING THE
RIGHT THING. I WAS SETTING HER AN EXAMPLE, BEING A LIBERATED
BUT LOVING MOTHER.

And Bob, in his haste to get to her, to help her, had
walked across the freshly cut lawn instead of using the path.
Sometimes she under-estimated him. Grass cuttings were easy
to clean up. When this thing with Dori was settled . . . When
Dori returned. She sighed as her mind became a sudden col-
lage of letters to Ann Landers and travel brochures. A week
away together. Time alone. Had it come to that then?

So Dori had gone to the Weibs! Old friends, whatever
that meant. People one liked and shared memories with. The
affection had been tinged with a slight superiority lately
because Brian Weib had been thrown out of university in his
first year and because Debbi, age-twin to Dori, had needed an
abortion at only seventeen.

Why had Dori gone there? How could she tolerate their

totalitarian establishment views when she was used to enlight-
ened liberalism with her toast and jam at home?

Bob set two cups on the tray, with saucers. She liked saucers. Sugar and milk. The doctor liked sugar. She liked coffee.
Drank so much of it her hands were beginning to turn brown.
Caffeine. A drug, doctor. Keeps you slim and shaky. But in
times of communion, times of family stress, the drink was tea.
He carried the tray into the room ceremoniously, wondering
whether there were male geisha now for tired Japanese business ladies, and was met by her words.

"When Sophie Weib called, she said Dori didn't want to
talk right now but would in a day or two. And I'm her
mother."

Another primeval wail: I am her mother. I am his wife. I
am her husband. She is my daughter. This is our son. Meet
our dog, Tom. They are our friends.

Correct the above sentences.

"There's nothing we can do right now. This happens to
everybody. And we can't live their lives for them."

"But what did she mean, 'irregular'?"

"Kids use long words sometimes without knowing what
they mean."

" 'Irregular' isn't particularly long."

"She'll come back."

"Meanwhile her room's empty. Her friends will call. I'll
have to say something to the neighbours when they want her
to baby-sit."

"Fuck the neighbours."

There was a silence. Martha was not one for picking up a
chance at a quick come-back. She did not say, 'Isn't one of us
doing that enough'. And in any case, she did not, must not,
could not, know.

The silence was like a crystal, smooth and opaque, unsul-
lied by word or sound. If people only still believed in the great

god Sigmund, they would have labelled that a classic error. But she said nothing. Besides she could not know.

But the silence was not total or real. In the kitchen a tap dripped. From downstairs came the sound of Sam's record player. The true silence was only between them.

She stirred her tea.

He sat down, balancing his cup like an infrequent visitor.

"Your plants are thriving," he remarked.

"Yes, aren't they," she replied.

"I'll have to go back to the office. But maybe you'd like dinner out."

"Not tonight. Thank you."

They stirred and sat and sipped and said nothing. Like a stranger in the room, he admired the vivid painting above the mantelpiece, an original by an unknown young artist who believed in colour but not at all in form. The upholstery on the two chairs either side of the fireplace needed cleaning. There must be a way to get the dirt off without sending them, expensively, to be cleaned. The recently re-covered loveseat made the chairs seem shabbier than they actually were. It was not a habit of Martha's to allow anything to show signs of dirt or wear. Were there other ways in which, imperceptibly to him, she was changing? Had Dori become aware of it?

"You've been working too hard," he said.

"And neglecting everything? And everybody?"

"That wasn't what I meant. Soapy water will soon get the dirt off, I suppose."

"Leave me alone. I'll be all right in a while. I have to get used to the idea of Dori being — independent."

This was the Martha Murray of record whose summer camp training had taught her how to deal with success but not with failure, with righteousness but not with guilt, with the image in the mirror but not what lay behind it; and whose own distrust of all the lessons had led her to pick a farmer's boy for a husband. Slowly she would gather herself together. Slowly and with determination. But it wouldn't be easy.

The courting of Martha hadn't been easy. One night after a starchy evening at their house, this house, when names had been dropped and references to great occasions made — 'but Bob won't know about that, dear' — he had taken a slight revenge. Stopping his battered old car at the end of Chellow Street, he had reached over for the basket of peaches, a gift from his father for the Murrays which he could not bring himself to deliver ('How very sweet of Mr. Ferrand') and had softened them in his hands before throwing them hard so that they landed on doors and walls and sidewalk with a comforting splat.

He had, though, enjoyed being seen out with the small and dainty medical student. Good manners. Small appetite. 'May I speak to Martha?' 'Just a moment, Mr. Ferrand.' And then, loudly, 'It's that boy from Niagara.' The tone in their voices hadn't deterred him. He had marched along, striding over them, to the wedding day. The Wedding Day when his father had let the soil drift through his fingers and his mother, regally, had watched all these shallow city-dwellers and found them wanting and shed a tear for her lost son.

Desperately he wanted to say to his wife, now, 'But it's been good, hasn't it, Martha? It has all been worth it, hasn't it? Martha? It has to have been, eh, Martha?' But he dared not pose the questions in case she wanted answers in return.

"And there was the dry cleaner," she said.

"The dry cleaner?"

"He brought me the wrong dress. A peculiar, slinky black thing. 'This isn't mine', I told him. 'I don't wear things like this.' 'Perhaps you should,' he said, and pushed it in the door. And later on a woman phoned and said, 'I'm Elsa Kwan.' And I told her I had her dress by mistake — that's the name on the ticket — and she said, 'Keep it' and hung up. Never did tell me what she wanted. I don't understand."

So THEY were using the dry cleaner as a messenger, a deliverer of hints and truths. There was nothing THEY didn't know. It was like a gigantic ant hill. THEY were watching it.

Reporting on it. Manipulating the ants.

"I don't understand it," Martha was saying. "So many strange things happening all at once. Dori. The dry cleaner. And yesterday, when I went out, I bumped into the mailman by mistake. He pushed me away quickly but I could see there were eggs and milk in his bag. Eggs and milk!"

"Maybe he helps the milkman out sometimes. Maybe he says you take the letters to fifteen and seventeen and I'll take the eggs and milk to twenty-one and twenty-three."

She was looking at him, frowning, the two lines down the centre of her forehead marked there forever now. To dispel his flippancy she said, "We shan't need so much milk with Dori away."

Milk and cookies after school. Eternally. They stopped sucking mother's milk but then forever after the comfort of milk and cookies was their prerogative. After school. At bedtime. A long stream of milk swishing them towards death.

"I'd better be getting back."

"I shouldn't have called you at work."

He looked at her across the silence and across the wide river of milk. They had, the two of them, arm-in-arm, high-stepped out of university; those most likely to achieve everything. And the buoyancy that had carried them along had made it easy to ignore the older Murrays with their superior turned down mouths, their frequent and vivid recollections of late, great personages and grand, high-style living. He had refused to touch his forelock to them.

But the coiled spring in them which was supposed to propel Martha and Robert Ferrand to the Top had only been a kind of youthful high spirits on his part and the excitement of living in the city; a distance from the orchards. For her it was a female fervor, a mixture of emotional and sexual drive which remained tense and viable in some women to the end of their lives ('and now Miss Tisha Knight, an incredible sixty-five year old', as on to the screen walks a Ph.D. in a silver lame gown slit up to the thigh showing long, good legs and not a sign of a metal hip joint), but in Martha it had dwindled to a firm, competent quietness. She was a woman who noticed that the mailman had butter and eggs in his bag.

"It's as if everything has turned hostile," she said, waving her arm to include the world of which she had till now been a recognised and card-carrying member. There was the place on the wall where, in her parents' reign, her graduation picture had hung. In the street outside, familiar with known faces, even the trees spelt security and the greenery of the Quinns' overgrown garden was not a dark forest but part of a favourite landscape. Beyond the end of Chellow Street lay a city which had always treated her kindly.

And Bob who had for all these years thought of himself as Adam began to wonder if he was not instead the serpent in her Garden.

The Reverend Cline was sitting in his garden enjoying the evening sun. A large panama hat shaded his face. He had bought the hat in Jerusalem and liked to think it lent him a holier aura. Looking out from under it, he felt like a saint in a stained glass window carrying his own halo everywhere he went. He saw the world with kinder eyes.

He waved to Dr. Ferrand as she rushed to get into her car and drive down to the hospital. A neat small woman. She was not his type. She had probably never had much flesh on her and must, in any case, be at least forty by now. What a pity she had thrown herself away on that half-French philanderer from nowhere. The neighbours said that his parents had driven to the wedding in a farm van and had spent the whole of the reception digging up the garden and re-arranging the trees.

Well nothing good had ever come out of Quebec. Except of course for little Solange. And then, too, poor Simone. Cute little accents they had. But aside from them, nothing. The sooner Quebec seceded, the better. It was nothing but a source of strikes and unrest; a deep well into which the Federal Government was forced to pour money. His money. A sample poll taken on Chellow Street would find every man and woman in favour of quick separation.

Looking down at the pile of bills in his hand, he knew that he had been right to call the travel agent. The Reverend Cline would have liked a rest. He had earned one. It would have been nice to spend a pleasant few weeks cutting off the dead roses, sitting here with a long drink in his hand, watching the world go by. Praying a bit. Catching up on his reading. Cherishing a few young and tender plants.

The travel agent had been willing. Impertinent but willing.

'Sure,' he had said, 'as soon as I can round up a flock. Getting a bit greedy, are we, Reverend. One of the seven deadlies, isn't it? Pride. Greed. Lust. I can only ever remember six. And when I'm doing my crossword it's always the other six. Just my little joke. I'll see what I can do. What's good for you is good for me. I'll call you when I've got a firm date.'

He looked down again at the bills, 'Emerald necklace and earrings — sixteen hundred dollars.' Jeannie liked emeralds. They were her birthstone. She looked beautiful in them and there was nothing she wouldn't do for him. They were expensive, but only a fraction of the price of the Persian rug.

'In ten years from now, this carpet will be worth twice as much,' the greasy stranger had said when he delivered it. 'Look at that,' he had continued, unrolling a corner of it. 'Beautiful.' And he had gone away in the night with a cheque for fifty thousand dollars.

The Reverend Cline had sat and looked at the rug for a long time, waiting for that beauty which had brought a moist gleam to the eye of the dago salesman in Iran, to strike him too, to fill him with joy and wonder, to make him leap about and cry out with pleasure. But though he looked at the faded browns and blues for fifteen minutes and searched the pattern for ancient and marvellous secrets, nothing stirred in him. The world was not altered for him through this purchase. Except that in ten years it would be worth a hundred thousand dollars and Quebec was not going to see one cent of it. The rug, lying there, was an appreciating and quite unshared treasure.

Jade was quite another thing. He had seen the piece that should fit in the alcove in the study. With a pale light behind it, it would glow in its true mysterious and ever-changing colours, giving pleasure of a deep and inexpressible kind.

Worship of beautiful things was not sinful. It was not a subtraction from the tribute owed to God. One worshipped the Almighty through beauty. Had not man, God's creation, worked on these things? How then could man despise what God, through man, had created? Every time a man or woman admired a painting, a sculpture, a carving, he or she was offering up a prayer to Him.

The old ladies liked that line. It drove them out of their hotel rooms to seek the most expensive rugs and figurines and jewels in the marketplaces of the East and pushed his commission up to four figures a trip. Not enough to make the trip worthwhile but a nice little bit of pocket money which was entirely his.

There was a bill from the nursing home and a note from the doctor: Your wife is doing very well, She wonders why you haven't been to see her. Perhaps you would be so good as to come on Friday at three p.m. You will be delighted to know that she should be well enough to come home by then. It is imperative however that you keep all liquor away from her. We can discuss this when we meet on Friday.

The doctor was one of those crazy eternal optimists. A fine quality. No doubt his work would be impossible without it. But Imelda was an alcoholic. If he didn't keep her secret hiding place stocked with forty-ouncers of rye, she would go to embarrassing lengths to get it. She had even, on one occasion, gone round to the Quinns' with a cup, to borrow some. He sighed. The mate of one so afflicted should be an object of pity. The tragedy of another's wasted life was not an easy cross to bear.

Generally the people who lived on Chellow Street had accepted him easily. If they had known of his struggle, the first whispered words at the Christmas Bazaar, the effort he had made *not* to accept that particular offer, they would have treated him with even more respect. But the sacrifice had to be made, if only for Imelda's sake.

The neighbours had welcomed a clergyman in their midst and his masters said it was the perfect connection. What THEY did with the stuff after he brought it back was no affair of his. Was it? It was a business transaction. An errand he did for a fee. No customs man ever asked to look in the Reverend Cline's extra bag. He never looked inside it himself. So it was no affair of his. Was it?

'And I say to you,' the loud, hollow voice called down, 'that whatsoever ye do unto the least of these, that ye do also unto me.' Had the arm once been naked? Was it wearing the long white lawn sleeve now to cover needle marks? A convulsion shook the Reverend Cline's body, something like a sob came out of him and his heart leapt in a fearful way.

" 'All things bright and beautiful,' " he began to sing softly. It was his soothing song, his lullaby. " 'All things great and small. . . .' " He knew the words of most hymns: 'Onward Christian soldiers', 'Oh God our help', his favourite; 'Jesus loves me, that I know.' In his childhood they had persuaded him to go to Sunday School by giving him a large coloured bead for each class attended. For years he had treasured the beads and kept them safe in a box by his bed. For years he had been happy in the certainty that one day he would be able to trade the beads for a marvellous prize. But the end of June came round relentlessly, time after time, and no one came to count his beads and proclaim him the winner. They had only, and without much fanfare, given him a book with coloured pictures in it.

Only Rocco, so much later, had offered him any sort of prize; a promise of wealth and an opportunity to pursue his studies of the History of Those Times. A scholarship.

Like a mosquito in a dark room, the thought nagged his mind that Rocco had shown him the view from the mountain, had said, 'All this can be yours' and that, because of the beads, he had accepted the visible reward and in so doing lost a much greater one.

The roses were doing particularly well in spite of the heat. It was never too late to reform. Never. Not even up to the last moment of all. He needed to spray them though. The green fly was a persistent little bastard. And the reformed sinner often got a better deal than the straight-all-the-time good guy. It was merely a matter of walking into the nearest police station. There was one at Charles and Jarvis. Better yet he could make a phone call. Next year a blue rose or two would make a nice addition. Rocco need never know. It was not as though they had him followed. They trusted him. Because . . . because of all the shit which they knew would fall on his head even should he open the door a tiny, tiny crack.

The Ferrands' door opened again and out came the farmer's boy. Ferrand could have stayed on the peninsula growing peaches usefully. Instead of that he chose to go about littering the landscape with dangerous nuclear power stations on the pretext of giving the world light. Did he not know that it had been done already!

He was coming up the path, stepping in the way of the sinking sun's rays, spoiling the evening.

"Your roses are lovely this year, Reverend."

"Thank you. Won't you sit down. Can I get you a drink?"

"No thanks. I can't stay. Didn't want to disturb you."

Wrinkled trousers in an era when the world was full of crease-free material, hair standing on end in the slight breeze, Ferrand was an ill-kempt specimen who had obviously suffered from acne in his youth and hadn't the manners to lower himself into a chair so that his host could talk and listen without strain. But what could you expect from a man who grew hollyhocks in a city garden? Hollyhocks were suitable only for planting round country outhouses. No doubt they made him feel at home. "How's your wife and the children?"

"Fine thanks."

Why didn't the oaf get on with it? If he wanted absolution from his adultery, he was in the wrong place. If he wanted help with a particular problem why didn't he come right out with it, take the soothing platitudes that would be offered him and go away. Rather than encourage him, the Reverend Cline waited quietly, saying nothing.

Finally his visitor spoke, "I've had a feeling lately that there's something wrong on Chellow Street."

It sounded like the first half of a code message to which he was supposed to reply with another cryptic phrase: 'The elk are migrating.' 'What a cold summer we've had.' 'I like spaghetti with meat sauce.' Instead he said, "The sprinkler's going to hit you in a minute."

Turning, Bob caught the arc of water on the front of his shirt. The shock of the cold water, even on such a warm evening, made him gasp.

"I'm sorry."

"That's all right. But I wonder if I might trouble you for a towel."

What kind of an intrusion was this? The fellow was only moments away from his own door. Steps away from his own bathroom. Was it a cunning way to get into his house? Was he in league with the tax people? Did he know that his host was programmed to give way to the importunate and to open doors when he was asked to do so.

"Certainly," he said, leading the way to the kitchen. "I'm afraid my housekeeping hasn't been up to much lately. The last housekeeper left without warning and I haven't found anybody yet."

"My wife has the same problem. Hard to find anybody

who'd get on with the work without supervision."

"Exactly." The Reverend Cline handed him the towel he used to dry the dishes with when he bothered to dry them. Most of the time he left the dishes to drain and, in their own time, they dried. If this fellow had only been a friend, a connoisseur, they might have sat together enjoying a glass of cognac and admiring the beauty of the Persian rug. To Ferrand it was most likely a thing that might have been ordered out of the catalogue.

"I wanted to come inside," he was saying, mopping at his chest with the towel, "because I can't help feeling that people are listening. It's as though somebody knows everything that goes on on Chellow Street."

"Really?"

"The other day, for instance, there was one of those detector vans parked near the Sopers. It said 'Home Delivery, Chinese Food' on it but anyone can stick a label on the side of a van."

"You think it's some Chinese gang?"

"No. I think it starts with the Paper Boy."

The Paper Boy! The man was out of his mind. Paranoid delusions. It happened every time. You move a man out of his class, a man who hasn't the intellectual stamina to cope with the change, and, every time, he thinks his surroundings are getting at him. "The Paper Boy?"

"I know you're up early too sometimes. And I wondered if you'd seen anything unusual. I've covered the hour between five and six on the five minutes and some of the threes but you might have been there when I wasn't."

"What are you getting at?" What was the bastard trying to tell him?

"Getting at? I was just wondering whether you'd seen the Paper Boy doing anything unusual."

"I can't say that I've noticed him. I'm usually on my way to Malton if I'm up early."

"No? Well if you do see anything, perhaps you'd let me

know. I'm keeping a kind of record." Bob wished now that he had not decided to come to the Reverend Cline. Water was seeping through his pants. The man was as shifty as hell. And in a situation like this it was not wise to trust anyone at all until the case was clear.

"I'll be off then."

"Yes."

"By the way," Bob said as he limped towards the gate, "I heard a terrible squeal at 5:54 this morning from over the road behind the Sopers."

"It was Fifi. She touched the coil of Sopers' new machine. My wife will be terribly upset."

At the mention of his wife, his eyes hooded over. Bob turned away reverently. As he walked home, he knew with certainty that the Reverend Cline had received a note too. It was apparent in his voice, in his shifty manner, in the way he had covered the papers on his lap. THEY were after him. Did THEIR prying eyes pierce the walls of all the houses on the street? The whole neighbourhood? The city?

The clergyman, watching him, frowned. Keeping a record was he? Officious little swine. 'Black Cadillac parked outside Cline's. 5:12 - 6:01.' Rocco ought to know about it. As the Ferrands' door closed, the Reverend Cline began to laugh. He laughed till his panama hat fell into his lap. He laughed silently and convulsively. In his mind there was a picture of a large cake being wheeled along Chellow Street; an armed man sprang out of it, blasting away up and down the street with his continuously firing gun, killing Ferrand, the Paper Boy, Soper the click-king, fat Mrs. Blue and her unpleasant dog. There were bodies everywhere and Mrs. Moxford's stole lay spread out on the sidewalk like a lovely, dead animal. He stopped laughing, and stopped letting the movie unroll, because when he looked closely at the crowded pavement, one of the bodies was his.

Walking home down Chellow Street had once been a pleasurable part of his day. The trees made a shady tunnel and the flowers in the gardens, hydrangeas, impatiens, delphiniums, roses, his own hollyhocks, bloomed in vivid contrast to the grass and to the stone or brick walls of the houses. The leafy tunnel loomed ahead of him now, dark and foreboding.

Bob had been making this same trip home for twelve years, ever since the Murrays had moved to an apartment in Vancouver. A move prompted, some said, by the unfortunate marriage made by their only daughter. It was a very unusual thing for anyone who lived in this part of the city to do. Like going to Florida, it was a kind of betrayal. If one was truly of the old guard one stayed and faced the horrible, damn cold winters and smiled and stayed in through old age, or used a walking stick, or slipped on the ice and suffered a broken hip, to die, stoically, of ice and snow and subhuman temperatures.

But the Murrays had gone West. For the first few years they had come back every six months or so to check that the house hadn't been allowed to deteriorate and disgrace the neighbourhood, and that the garden hadn't been turned into a corn patch. Then they had grown tired of the long journeys and stopped coming. They wrote infrequent letters marked by a lack of interest in Chellow Street and even in the family itself. Their new garden bloomed for nine months of the year and took up a great deal of their time.

Bob had never noticed before that some of the cement on which he trod twice daily was stamped, 'City 1956'. He stopped for a second and examined the slab on which he was standing. Further on, a brand new piece of paving was marked, 'Replaced 1976'. Further still, the date was 1946. An average of twenty-five years to wear out a sidewalk? How much contribution towards the wear and tear did one medium-sized man make treading the same path for twelve years? Walking, when he stopped to consider, nearly always on the same line, two-thirds of the way towards the outer edge of the sidewalk. There were red crosses painted on the water stop-cocks. Green crosses on the gas ones. Twigs and dogshit decorated his path in a random arrangement. A pretty, wilted corsage lay in the gutter as though a girl had endured an evening out with an oafish boy and thrown the flower aside as soon as she got home.

"Look where you're going, eh!" The boy on the skate board travelled dangerously close, went down over the curb, crossed the road, rode up the other side using his feet skilfully to guide the tiny vehicle up and around his own driveway to stop with a flourish at the front door. The boy's face was flushed with triumph. A skate board now. A surf board tomorrow. Summers in California. And somewhere downtown the happy boy's father no doubt worked his ass off to keep together a failing business; a struggle that none of his family appreciated.

Like Sam. Sam the tall student who was going up North for the weekend to water-ski and drink beer with his friends who were all careful not to throw their beer cans into the still lakes of Muskoka. Sam with the bright eyes and scornful look. Sam. When anyone said 'Sam', it was the look rather than the whole face which came into his mind. Sam thought that what his father did downtown was evil; evil as pyramid-selling, evil as piracy, evil as short-trading, as dealing in shoddy goods, watered wine, diluted drugs, and as throwing beer cans into clean lakes.

Their argument was long since over. It had only become repetitive. Each could have taken the other's side like protagonists in a long-running play. Martha could have acted as prompter and Dori as time-keeper. None of them needed a script.

Sam enters left, not smiling, and goes into his atmosphere-future-monster-children routine. Bob, not looking up from the newspaper, counters, with hysterical nonsense — read the figures — reasonably priced electricity — good employment — no accidents so far — what about coal miners. Sam speaks on behalf of windmills and solar energy. Taking out his folding easel and blackboard from his inside pocket, Bob draws a picture of windmills covering the surface of the province; the huge, striding flails far more ugly than any mill chimney or nice, round reactor building. Pulling his talking calculator out of another pocket, he lets it speak, in its clipped Martian accent, of the costs of solar energy and the fact that still, with solar energy used in each house, the load on the local generating station would be excessive at peak times. The sun does not always shine, my son, and storage tanks are huge. Thus the arguments have become

> Repetitive
> Non-productive
> Except of hostility.

Sam's side, those who called themselves environmentalists, was winning temporary victories. The giant stalling processes going on in government offices were making ripples that caused layoffs in all kinds of ancillary industries. At least, Mercer had said after the hearing, we have work in Calgary.

The hearing room itself had been a boobytrap of cables and electronic machinery. The words were being taped, the proceedings video-taped, the projected slides photographed and the words recorded also on dictaphones. Nothing of these meetings would be lost. Would you care to see the unexpurgated edition of the 1976 Energy Hearings? They run for four months and seven days with sanity breaks. Free copies of the text? Signed pictures of all the leading players? And next year, Marcel Marceau himself will reproduce it all in mime.

Not content with writing his findings down and binding them into heavy copies with large print for all to read, the young lawyer who seemed to have taken over the energy policy of the province was reading each page aloud and his mate was projecting his graphs and slides on to a screen at the front of the room.

The room itself had become a hypnotic machine. The constant whirring and clicking, the dimmed lights, the sound of a voice that has settled to a monotone because it knows it will be speaking for a long time and that no one is listening, all worked to produce torpor. There was relief when a messenger came in and whispered to one of the politicians seconded to the committee; he could then get up and leave, importantly and noisily, to attend to the wants of a constituent or another group. Everybody could shuffle and look round and the committee members had a chance to jiggle the ice on their water jugs.

The young lawyer had continued, "And document A-45, a submission by Mr. A. Marcus, shall from henceforth be known as A-46 and shall be titled, "A submission by Mr. A. Marcus."" Droning on, the voice listed sources and spoke with pride of the two thousand people who had been interviewed, the ninety-three meetings so far held, the forty-three important issues raised. Were they dead, then? was Bob's dying question. When he came to, half an hour, later, the voice was still at it and when the technician behind them changed tapes on his machine, he murmured for its benefit and with some incredulity, 'This is still Gerry Green speaking.'

If nothing else it was a tribute to the education system which had trained these people to sit in small rooms listening to dull speeches day after day. At school, each succeeding year brought longer lectures. At University, hour after hour was spent listening and the student who survived only did so because he knew that one day, with his degree in his hand, he would be doing the talking. He would graduate from being the Ear to become the Voice.

Bob felt Mercer grow tense beside him as the young man continued to speak highly of the recommendations he had worked out for the benefit of these sleepy politicians: If we flatten this curve on the graph here, slide number fourteen please Fred, higher up, yes, that's it, and bend this one slightly up, this gives us the equation 23. And it proves if you follow this line here that we cancel project A and project B we can save the taxpayer billions of dollars. The politicians woke up. That was their kind of talk.

Mercer shrieked a kind of tortured animal yell and jumped to his feet. "Oh yes," he shouted. "And what do you know about it? Oh yes. Let the poor bugger sit in the dark, unemployed, but for God's sake save him money. Nothing decent to eat but let's save him money. No place for the poor sod to go because there's no gas but let's save him money. Don't come crying to us when your bloody lights go out."

A power failure, total darkness so that he and Mercer could slink away, did not happen. A uniformed official tapped Mercer on the shoulder. He was pale and out of breath and, for the moment, incapable of further violence. The lawyer went on smoothly, "This is of course only a recommendation. The time for discussion will come later."

"Recommendation. Discussion. My ass," Mercer said. And they had left then, quietly, and let the machinery of democracy grind on in peace.

A black squirrel crossed his path, enjoying its happy summertime, darting across the road and back, rushing up the oak tree outside the Moxford's and looking down at him scornfully. From the Moxford's top window, a few pieces of paper fluttered down to earth. They looked like mutilated paper dolls. She was lying there now in the skylit room, naked on her stole, cutting out row after row of paper dolls and never, ever, getting them quite right. Excuse me madam, I have long been an expert at origami. There is nothing I cannot do with a sheet of old newspaper and a pair of scissors. Allow me.

At the side of the Towne Maison, the milkman was hovering. At this hour? Delivering some forgotten thing? Collecting the blackmail money? Taking more of his photographs with that ingenious, milk-carton-shaped camera?

"Mr. Ferrand? Mr. Ferrand?"

He turned to find the Quinn's daughter approaching him, pantherlike, from behind. "Hello."

"Hello Mr. Ferrand." She seemed to like saying his name. Not sure whether to call her Marianne or Ms. Quinn, he stood still.

"It's a lovely day," he said.

"A hot and harsh day."

"Nice under the trees." She was wearing cut-off shorts and he wished she would turn round so that he could see how short they were. Her legs were like young trees, planted there, rooted in those battered thong sandals. A T-shirt with YOU! printed on it cried out for an answer. "Are you still going to U. of T.?"

"No."

"I thought not. I haven't seen you around — going to school — walking by — for quite a few weeks."

"You noticed!"

"I didn't notice so much as — when you mentioned it — I realised."

Did Dori, whose young face now superimposed itself over the bright mask of this tall girl, talk to strange men like this, luring them into tongue-tied responses and fumbling replies? And provoking them perhaps into action? "My daughter starts at Waterloo in September."

"She should get a bike."

"She has one but never rides it."

She thought: his eyes are lined with dark rings around them. What other kind of worries could he have besides the very ordinary one of his wife finding out about his mistress?

He thought: she will offer to talk to Dori, to be an older sister maybe. This was her reason for stopping him on the street and practically laying her hand on his arm but not quite.

— He wasn't even running to fat yet. And didn't drink a great deal. One could easily tell who were the drinkers on the street merely by watching the times at which they came and went, and by knowing in which houses dinner was served late and carelessly.

— She could be a late developer. No wonder, in that peculiar household. Probably, in a year or two, she would get involved in charitable works or even politics.

— If you treat a man for too long as though he is an ordinary man, he will become one. This man had latent passion lying in a deep dark pool in his soul. A touch, which even Elsa Kwan did not have, could ignite it.

— She should get out of that house into a healthier atmosphere.

— He needed to be free of all that crummy domesticity.

— She should have a nice little apartment.

— He should have a place downtown.

"What are you doing now?" he asked, noticing that they had moved and were now standing in front of his own house.

"I'm quite satisfied with my life. It has become symbiotic and green is a perfect colour for it. I'm standing here, trying to cope with a sentence I read today, 'Behind every man stand thirty ghosts.' Some of yours are showing, Mr. Ferrand. I am aware of other people's ghosts."

"Are you?"

"I could have been a dancer. My grandmother dances. Or a builder. My great-grandfather built things. Or a scholar. They said so. But I didn't choose to."

"What do you choose to do?"

"I'm not a virgin, Mr. Ferrand. And I know that you screw around."

The pink scarf round her neck was caught by a breeze and drifted lightly to one side; the shorts were a screaming invitation. She stared at him with a bland wide-eyed look that suggested she had put her toys away and stopped collecting wild flowers and would never again make a leaf collection for teacher and that Dick and Jane had been replaced forever by Colette and Mellors who neither ran to be seen nor bowled hoops.

He tried to look to either side but her eyes held him. They were knowing eyes. They knew everything in the world;

and nothing. They had been shown all that there ever was to know; and seen none of it. They had met all shapes of good and bad and had recognised none of them.

"I'm working on a book of poems," she said. "My publisher says they're going to be a sensation."

"That's great. You should meet my son, Sam. He writes poetry."

"I'm not interested in very young men."

As she walked away, he watched her hips. She had taken off the chiffon scarf and was holding it high, letting it float over the Cline's roses. A moment later she came back towards him.

"Well," she said, before turning and drifting off again, "do you think fifty dollars is about right?"

Christ, he said to himself. Christ! What was that all about? Knowing exactly what it was all about, his mind full of shattered images and broken glass, he heard Martha's voice calling to him from the front door.

"The phone, Bob. You're wanted on the phone."

As she turned and went into the Quinn's jungly garden, the girl made a sign at him, holding up five fingers of one hand and forming an 0 with the thumb and forefinger of the other.

A disembodied voice came at him through the hedge, close to his ear. "Interesting, Mr. F. Very. And you haven't paid up on the last one yet. Have you? I would if I was you."

'Time of garbage pick-up in this area has changed. Garbage must now be put out before 7 a.m. Garbage cans must be taken in immediately after pick-up so as not to leave the street looking unsightly.'

69

"Did you get one of these notices? Who do they think they are? Anybody'd think we live in a Public Housing Project."

The minutes of the Council Meeting referred in glowing terms to that district which had been a fine residential area *ab urbe condita* and in which large trees flourished and people lived in peace and harmony with their surroundings. There was no need, the minutes continued, for these fine residents to get excited about the development of Lippert Boulevard into an arterial road. It was unlikely that this would ever take place. And if it did, it would not be for another year. In any case, the plans were still on the drawing board. Nothing was final. Fine residents in other areas who had at first fought tooth and claw against such a change had later found it delightful to have a main road close by as it brought trade and life and strangers and money to the neighbourhood. (An objection by an intransigent Very Conservative Member that the first fine residents had become a different lot of people by the time the road went through — tradesmen who had bought up the fine residences of the aforementioned fine residents — was hooted down and not mentioned in the minutes.)

Marianne had listened to it all carefully and had tried to make notes in her own shorthand. Once or twice she had wanted to speak but they had made it clear that minutes were no business of the public's. Later they had begun to talk with boring accuracy about the amount of money that could be saved if coffee was drunk only in the mornings and the members brought their own for the afternoons in flasks.

"I am making an effort," she said to Henry-the-analyst. She had always refused to lie on his couch. She could lie quite well in his chair. "I'm not lying to you now. I am trying out several jobs to see which I like. I realise that if I'm going to write worthwhile poetry, I must be involved in life itself. So I'm looking for life. ITSELF."

"Great, Marianne. I'm very pleased. But are you looking in the right places?"

"If you ask questions and raise obstacles, doctor, I won't be able to continue."

"I thought we'd paid the paper boy this week?"

"Paid him about six weeks in advance."

"Well he's here again."

"Paging Dr. Ferrand. Dr. Ferrand please come to Emergency." Martha hurried to find a child lying on a table, surrounded by limpid Muzak. A bright shining boy with a broken leg or maybe two. A skate board. After dark. Yes, his distraught parents had told him not to but they couldn't keep him off it. Of course it had no lights. The driver, hysterical in the outer room, was in no way to blame.

Eaton's was advertising lawnmowers. Shiny yellow riding lawnmowers suitable for several acres of grass on a small farm. Illustrated leaflets showing to advantage each glossy nut and bolt were distributed only on those city streets where the inhabitants might be expected to have enough money in the bank to spend on such toys. The boy delivering the flyers with their kindly offer of a free demonstration anywhere within a thirty mile radius, had found many friends and diversions on his route and did not arrive on Chellow Street until it was almost dark. Whistling to keep the ghosts at bay, he put the leaflets in mailboxes where there were mailboxes and in milkboxes where there were not. He had been strongly admonished against leaving them on porches to get wet or to blow away in the wind. He wondered whether the $15.99 he found in one milkbox was a tip or the prize at the end of a treasure hunt.

The men gathered in the room were olive-skinned although they spent a great deal of their time indoors. One of them was carefully tilting a longnecked bottle as he held a lighted candle over it and let the red wax dribble down the glass to make an attractive pattern.

"D'you think Cline'll skip out on us?"

"He's in too deep."

"He's a little man. Likes big money."

"We'd know if he was doing a bunk. Before he did!"

"Goddam right."

"That wax is dripping on the rug, dummy."

"Is the pound still falling?"

"The dollar is."

"What do you think they'll call their money in Quebec? Dollars or francs?"

" 'You have to believe me, officer,' this little old lady said. 'It's all true. I saw the whole exchange.' I said to her what we always say: We'll take care of it right away, lady. Thank you very much for thinking of us.

So I look the guy up and he lives on Chellow Street for Christ's sake. A clergyman. Respectable as hell. Some of these old girls, they stop having sex, it all goes to their minds. If she calls, tell her we're investigating the matter and if anything turns up she'll be the first to know."

At the Energy Hearing today, Mr. David Harvin proved conclusively that not only is nuclear energy extremely dangerous, it is also unnecessary. There was no reason why, he said, that the whole country should not be turned into a rural paradise. People, when they get used to it, actually like to have to fetch water from lakes, to go to bed at dusk and to grow all their own needs with good, solid, iron-age implements. With this kind of living made compulsory, the need for power stations of any kind would gradually disappear. The Committee has urged the government to suspend all further development of power plants so that the Harvin Plan may be fully investigated.

"Do you think we should put six or seven, Johnson?"

"Six or seven what?"

"Time, darling."

"Whenever they'll eat and drink the least. Are you making it quite clear they have to go home for dinner?"

"It'll have to be outside. I haven't time to clean the house. My monograph is at a crucial stage."

"How did we get trapped into this party, anyway?"

"It was in the paper. That we were going to have one."

A man with deep terror in his eyes, blood seeping down the front of his torn shirt, was reaching towards the monster that pursued him. Slowly he backed into a corner, terrified, as the great creature with all its fur bristling came closer and closer with some of the man's blood already dripping from its teeth, and then, turning his profile to the camera, the man died.

"I thought Robert Redford was always the hero."

"So?"

"Heroes don't die. Robert Redford doesn't die."

"Sometimes they do. Anyway maybe they'll show him in heaven."

"Dummy. Who believes in that any more."

"Get some popcorn and shut up, eh? Look. He's moving."

"Summer make-up courses. We all know what that means. You're here taking it because you didn't make it during the year. Lazy or stupid or both. I'm here teaching it because I need the bloody money. Pedagogically we're all way down the fucking academic ladder. Right then. Let's get on with it and show the world we can fight back. You there. What's your name? Exactly what did you pick up from last year's Politics 120, so ably taught by my tenured colleague?"

"Sam Ferrand."

"What? Hold it right there. Have we an object lesson? Are you from Quebec?"

"No. My grandparents were."

"Ah."

"We learnt that politics was the art of the possible."

"Shit! And 'it's a dog eat dog world' and all that. Forget what you learnt last year and let's begin with the people's revolution."

"In China or Russia?"

"The world, man. The world."

'Rumour has it that a party is to be held before too long at the fine Quinn Mansions on Chellow Street. We predict that it will be the affair of the season. One of those grand old parties for which the Giant's home was once famous. There are those who remember the famous time when no fewer than sixteen people were lost for three days after a Quinn party. So hold your breath and wait for the mailman.'

"I don't know how your wife got back on to it so quickly, Reverend Cline. I really thought when we sent her home that she was much better. But as you say — where there's a will . . . I'm afraid we've had to put the fees up again, but I do give you our reduced rate for clergy wives. We too have our expenses you know."

"Do you see that sparrow there? The one with the white tail? I think it must be a mutant. There's nothing in my bird-book about sparrows with white tails. And of course with what's in the air nowadays, anything can be happening. They say there are already more deformed children than there ever used to be."

"What's that terrible noise, Marianne?"
"Granny practising her dance for the party."

Before leaving for a tour of the Middle East, the Energy Minister said that nothing was more certain than that, in the future, we must do everything we can to ensure the widest pos-sible consideration of every known source of energy and that he will on his return from the tour, form three new committees especially for this purpose.

> *Id-id-id-i-am-in*
> *Oh what a mess you're in*
> *Kenya has cut off your oil supply*
> *Don't come to me for help.*
"I don't think it'll make the charts."

"We can only wait. That's what a recession is all about, isn't it?"

Marianne: click. After I left him, I rushed up to my room

and looked out of the window to catch another glimpse of him; not my first lover but possibly my first client. He seemed to be standing there listening and then he made a grab at the hedge and pulled his hand back quickly because it's a twiggy hedge and must be very prickly. Then he ran into the house. My theory is that like knights of old, he was testing himself, saying to himself, 'If I can put my hand into this prickly hedge, quickly and suddenly, I shall know I have the strength to go to her. The girl, my new love.' The question is, has he got fifty dollars to spare? A man like that with a family and a house, needs a lot of money.

My mother has gone out of her mind over this party. Every day she invites more people. My father is talking of shooting himself the day after it, or pleading bankruptcy in the courts. I wonder which would make a better poem.

The immense question of the moment is, 'Shall I invite my publisher to the party? Would he be impressed or anti-impressed? He's a very quiet man and seemed, when he was here to lunch, to be in the grip of some terrible inner crisis.

"Id-id-id-i-am-in . . ."
"What's that awful row?"
"New song."
"Jesus!"

Delphiniums next year where the hydrangeas were now and move the fuchsia to the back and replace it with azaleas. Hydrangeas were boring — just went on being white or blue blobs day after day.

"Did you read where in France they caught up with an ex-SS man and killed him?"
"They don't let anyone live peacefully, do they?"

"They said he'd sent a lot of people to the gas chambers. That kind of thing."

"That was war, wasn't it? Everybody was doing it."

"Nobody forgets. It's a terrible world."

"At least we can watch the Olympics."

"Close the drapes. The light's spoiling the picture."

"How come every time we settle down to a drink in an evening, some bastard starts up a lawnmower? And that's a damn noisy one. We ought to get up a petition."

A man on a yellow riding mower was cutting the next-door garden methodically up and down, to the road and back to the house. His powerful blades were cutting down the flowers and his treads dug into the beds and his hooded engine hit the hedge each time he made a turn. Ginny Blue was watching from her window. Surely it was rather an ostentatious garden accessory. But if the neighbours wanted to spend their money on such noisy, unnecessary toys it was no affair of hers.

And then she screamed as she saw him drive straight through the hedge and make long, cropped paths across her garden. She rushed outside shouting, waving her arms and leaping about from side to side, trying to keep out of his way in her futile effort to stop him. Relentlessly he and his machine severed begonias and grass, small shrubs and Common Creeping Juniper. When he had finished, he drove off, the sound of the engine making him deaf to her pleas.

Sitting high on his seat majestically, he went away down the road leaving her weeping amidst the wreckage of her garden.

'Old Rosedale lady ravished.' For want of a mere seven letters and an apostrophe, the headline had become a disaster.

The editor of the local paper had yelled down the phone at six different people in his search for an 's' and a 'garden'. Tired now, his hand was shaking and his eyes filled with tears. The Blues were an old, established family. The Quinns too lived on that street. And below him, out of the window, was only a three-floor drop.

Part Three

Martha had been quite sincere in saying, "The emergency is here." She felt as if a clearer, truer path had been pointed out to her. She had been floundering, out there in the world, trying to help people who could get a dozen others to help them if they only called out, "Nurse. Doctor. Help." She had been fiddling about with bones and bandages like a soldier who pretends he is an expert at the telephone exchange because he doesn't want to be in the front line. (Deep down, she realised, she had always regarded that as the true heroism.)

What she had been ignoring, sidestepping, as she set off downtown in white coat and stethoscope, was the battle at home. Wounded bodies healed. Minds rarely did. It might not be too late. Even though, at this moment, she seemed to be looking up from the bottom of a damp pit with only a sliver of light shining down to help her. The sides were slippery and no one was offering her a ladder but nonetheless some kind of ascent must be tried.

She had fallen into the pit through believing blindly that the way was clear. Long ago they had said it was all a matter of having the right china, stapled together perhaps but expensively right; a man would not wander away from a house where the pile on the carpet was deep, where the right accents were heard and no raucous music ever played and the cream and sugar were served separately on a small tray. And, mentally at least, Bob had wandered. It was not like him to be abstract. Somewhere, walking through the woods, they had let go of each other's hands and were now separated by many, many trees. "YOU COULD SEE THE CRYSTAL PALACE IF IT WASN'T

England had lost its influence on Chellow Street in the last couple of decades. And Chellow Street had lost some of its security. The world Gerald Quinn and his friends had built was changing. Because they had closed their ranks and kept out all undesirables, whether people or ideas, they had thought themselves safe forever. But Johnson Quinn was not like his grandfather. The Moxfords had managed to slide their ugly wedge-shaped house in between the others. The garbagemen were now the dictators of times and arrangements. The dry cleaner was delivering his goods at random. Before long, the mailman would be reading the mail to decide whether it merited delivery or not.

On T.V. women of beauty and enchantment were offered to men of all ages. It was not enough any more to be clean and intelligent, there had also to be an element of surprise. "Yes," the writer to Ann Landers stated, "sometimes I greet my husband on his return from work wearing only a bikini, sometimes a long gown, sometimes nothing. He never knows what to expect." That's all right for California. In Canada cold blasts come in when the door is opened.

'I cannot offer you excitement,' she wanted to say to Bob who seemed to have built up his own diversion by inflating the deficiencies of the tradesmen into some kind of persecution fantasy. The attitudes of the workers were symptoms of a changing and shifting society and she could give him no nice pills to ward them off. So, because of a lack of imagination in her, 'sometimes I greet my husband wearing only a towel,' he now walked about like the Red Shadow, seeing enemies behind each shrub.

Definitely the male menopause was on him. He was young but there were no strict guidelines as to age. And there were the other, obvious signs; his lack of response, his defensiveness when spoken to, his uneasy replies to the woman on the phone, and the way he had stood there, on the street, sheepishly, talking to Marianne Quinn.

It could be that he was having a downtown intrigue. A man at his age exuded a certain pathos like a dog in heat. Maybe there was a girl at the office. A plumpish woman with soft hands who reached across the lunch table to touch him and whose soft curly hair, as he would never realise, was a wig.

And Carmen, in her flaming scarlet dress, tossed her long black mane and reached for the knife hidden in her bosom. She drew it out but before she could stab her unfaithful husband, she had performed on herself an instant and total mastectomy. The other diners refused to pay their bills and since the rug was ruined the restaurant went out of business.

So, be up to date, "interesting", for heaven's sake — how much more up to date could you be than among the bodies being wheeled into the emergency department — she read *Time* and *Newsweek* and *Maclean's* who served her adventurers and artists and an occasional hero.

Look at that Israeli colonel. A magazine article showing diagrams of the attack, had printed his picture and biography. How many women looking at his photograph would not fancy the idea of taking him out for an evening of silent communication? What need for words when there, sitting opposite you, was a hero, a man who, without giving a dime for his own life, went ahead and started small wars which might have world-shaking reverberations. 'I am an ordinary man,' he might say. But when he took off his clothes, there would be the tight-muscled body of a lean man always ready to fight, who was never caught unawares.

His face showed great strength. . . . And what was she, the pacifist, doing, sitting here admiring a killer, a man who went out and killed to prevent others being killed; the age-age-age-old excuse of war-makers and murderers. If she had been a Roman Catholic, she might have crossed herself now for making a tentative move towards the devil.

She would have liked at least a little of the Colonel's strength. She was going to need strength now. Like Indians in last century's forests, these problems had been stalking her, the unwary traveller, and now, they had pounced and scalped her.

And Sam the Spectator must be brought into the family again. He had taken to looking at them all from the outside in. There were embryo lines of cynicism forming round his mouth so that when he smiled it was not quite pleasant.

Below her, his music ceased. His footsteps came pounding up the stairs. In one movement he came across the kitchen and sank into the chair opposite her, looking instantly as though he had moulded himself into a peculiar shape around it and would never be separated from it again. At nineteen he knew everything, as she herself had known everything at that age; the rest had been a slow decline into ignorance.

"He has a lot of problems just now, Sam."

"Who doesn't!"

"Don't start on the argument as soon as he gets in."

"I've given up. We only say the same things over and over."

"How's your foot?"

He took off his sock and held the foot towards her. It was not clean, but the patches of yellowish skin were flaking away leaving clean, new skin underneath. "That stuff you gave me must work. It doesn't itch so much."

"Keep using it."

"Yes doctor."

Martha wanted to cry out, 'Why did she go to the Weibs, Sam,' as though he might have an answer. It shouldn't matter. The Weibs were friends. Friends were surrogate selves. One said to the world, 'Judge me, if you must, by these.' Instead she said, "We used to have good times with the Weibs."

"You did."

"You were there. You and Dori and their kids."

"Were we?"

The copper pans on the wall, the gleaming cupboards,

the sound of the lawnmower, all faded. The kids shrieking outside became other kids on another day, on a beach near Georgian Bay. In a small clearing stood the Weibs' cottage built by hand and with loving care. The lake stretched out before them into an unknown distance. The lake and the weekend. A long weekend. There had been a touch of paradise in sitting there, with these affectionate friends, the children happy, playing little games. There was sunshine and all kinds of talking to do. Later on, the children in bed, there was time to play bridge and to talk again.

"You had a good time," Sam, in the present, was saying.

They had gone swimming during the day and spent hours lying in the sun getting dry again. Playing with a beach ball. Laughing. Sometimes falling on the sand to reach the ball or collapsing with laughter at a hilarious remark.

"He's weird, Mr. Weib," Sam said, still in the present.

And the wine they had brought. Bottles of wine. Bob liked Beaujolais. The rest of them preferred Sauternes.

In the early evening, they walked along the beach, picking up driftwood, imagining it into real shapes. Sometimes just the three of them, Sophie and herself and Bob because Jon Weib liked to look after the children. He enjoyed putting them to bed, he said; it gave him a chance to know them. In the city he came home late from his psychiatrist's office and didn't see much of them. So he put all four of them to bed and told them stories while the walkers strolled along, talking about the changing aspects of their world and of marriage and of neighbourhoods. Temporarily they owned the world and disposed of it according to their mood. Fragments drifted back. Fragments of conversations that had made them feel philosophical and marvellous.

"If one comes to the right conclusion by recognition of the facts rather than. . . ."

"But it's a question of whether you think man is discoverable."

"Mysteriousness is only a protective sham and has nothing to do with truth."

If they had recorded those conversations and played them back to the people they were now, they would hardly understand what the words meant.

"I was afraid of him," Sam — in the kitchen — said.

She and Sophie used to take all the food to the cottage. Taking turns to prepare simple meals of ham and bread and cheese and salad. Cookies for the kids. A special Cottage Cake made of raisins and spices which would have tasted revolting in the city became a treat in this primitive wooden home. Part of their return to Nature. Cottage Cake.

"I didn't know why I was afraid of him at the time. Now I know that he was a sadist."

They had worn very few clothes. Now and then, the men, Bob and Jon, might look at the other wife and see most of her body. Like the spice in the Cottage Cake it startled them a little into a new kind of knowledge. But those were sexless days. There was no privacy. The beds weren't up to much. Hard bunks layered round the walls to save space.

"You were drunk a lot of the time, Ma."

And then Bob had begun to want to leave early, on the Sunday instead of the Monday. To beat the traffic, he said. As though he wasn't enjoying it any longer. And she began to doubt that he ever had. It was a game of playing house, of roughing it in the bush, peculiar to certain types and families who spent their winters planning for it. Well-to-do middle class men died building their primitive dwellings. They spent ten months in a sedentary job and then, on the first fine weekend, rushed Up North to cart boatloads of rocks about, to fell trees and move giant beams. Victims. Statistics. Over this holiday weekend twenty-five people were killed on the highways. Seven were drowned. Three struck by lightning. (The fools would stand under a tree.) One farmer gored by his bull. And no one mentioned the heart attacks which felled the would-be pioneers. Very natural causes.

"You hardly noticed us."

It had all come suddenly to an end anyway. About ten years ago. Toby Weib had nearly drowned and they had lost him for five hours while he was clinging to the upturned canoe in which, although forbidden to do so, he had gone out alone. She and Sophie had spent all of those hours staring out at the lake, waiting for a glimpse, a shadow, the sound of the searching motor boat returning with Toby in it, alive.

After that Jon Weib, in a fit of anger, had sold the cottage; and never taken his family on holiday again. So there had been no more singing in the moonlight, softly, so as not to wake the kids.

"He used to make us dive down in the deep water. Told us that the clean water was at the bottom. Boys had to be tough. Not afraid. When he put us to bed those nights he told us stories that kept us shivering with fright under the covers. None of us dared move. And when the girls cried out, he'd hug them and cuddle them to make them feel better. I hated him."

"What did you say, Sam?"

"Nothing, Ma."

"They were good times, weren't they?"

She looked at him. Her son the doctor — lawyer — Indian Chief. His hair not too long but neatly trimmed at the nape of his neck. He would be a vainer man than his father was but none the worse for that.

"How's summer school?"

"I'm not crazy about it."

"Well. . . ."

"It's O.K. ma. O.K. I'll keep going. Stop trying to make everything nice."

"I just wish Dori hadn't gone away."

"She'll be back."

"What are you doing at school?"

"Today we talked about India."

"I was reading about those new measures in the paper. Time they did something drastic. They just don't seem to manage any other way."

"But it's repressive, Ma. Dictatorship."

"It's a huge country. Maybe there's no other way just now."

"Oh Ma. That's the Old Toronto Fascist in you talking. Do you think that in a while, when things are better, it'll be easy to get rid of the dictatorship? Just like that?"

"I'm only saying it's a good way, right now, to prevent huge numbers of people from starving."

"Compulsory vasectomy!"

She looked at him, the freedom fighter, loving him. It was sad that he would change soon, accept certain things, learn to compromise. "What was that noise?"

"I think it was Dad. Looked in and went on into the living room."

Martha knew that Bob had crept by, on into the den beyond the living room, to sit in his soft chair, put up his feet on the footstool her mother had embroidered long ago for another pair of feet, and spread out his newspaper as a screen between himself and the rest of the house.

Bob set down the glass. It was time now to go and look for the enemy out there. For the past twenty minutes THEY had been tapping at the window, disturbing his annual wine-tasting. He had been comparing, as a lover of both, his father's two-year-old peach wine and a '69 Chauvenet. The peach wine had won as it always did at this time of year, and he had almost emptied the bottle. It had a powerful bouquet that brought with it the strong odour of summer orchards and dry fields and furtive love-making. And it was good.

A louder sound outside made him go for a stick and a flashlight and march out to war. Nothing had happened. Bob flicked the flashlight on and sent a small circle of light flickering over the milkbox, the wall, the pathway beside the house.

Nothing had moved. Nothing had changed. It was two o'clock and pitch dark. The trees were swaying like so many menacing hands reaching out to touch him.

'I am here,' The Great Elm was murmuring, 'because in my human shape I lewdly chased young girls and ever since have been rooted to this spot. The things I know. The things I've seen. But my time is a-a-a-lmost up.' It gave a swaying wail and drew back as the other trees shuddered an answering chorus.

Safe in their houses all the people in Chellow Street lay in bed asleep or listening to the wind, complacently accepting the corruption around them and not wanting to expose it in case it touched their own lives and held them up to public view: $1.50 a time. Cheaper than tigers and more fun than pterodactyls. Come, see the two-legged monsters.

He grasped his walking stick more tightly round the middle. He was ready now to attack any intruder, to beat the blackmailer of Chellow Street with his calculating notes, his mean demand.

There was a sizzling hiss and a screech from the Soper's backyard and a second later, a black cat, all its hair on end, bounded across his path. Harris's new, improved trap needed still more improvement. The first spits of rain began to fall on his head and he wished the walking stick was an umbrella. It was not friendly summer rain but the kind that would, in a moment, come swamping down over everything. He knew now what he had to do. He must go in and put on a clean shirt and drive down to the hospital and say, 'I need my wife. This is an emergency.' He must beat down their doors if need be, set himself on a trolley and lie there in wait for her. 'Doctor, I need you,' he would cry out. And, recognising his need, she would lock the door and say, 'hold all calls' and give him what he wanted.

He went to the porch and pushed the front door. It remained firmly closed. He knew without looking that there was no key in his pocket. All the contents from all his pockets were on the dresser top in their bedroom.

He stood there, cursing. Elsa, hospitable but perhaps "not at home" couldn't be reached before this downpour came at him. He looked up and down the street for a hope of shelter. Faint glows showed where the nervous sleepers lay. The only house with bright lights on was the Quinn's. 'Excuse me, Mrs. Quinn, I was out for a walk and the rain came on. . . .' Tall and solid, their house stood there on its own at the end of the street, a guardian, a manor house, an example to struggling peasants (you too can have one of these if you work hard and are thrifty and don't mind the hours), but not a shelter. He looked up at the tower room where he knew she sat. Was she there now, awake, entwined in chiffon scarves, taking them off slowly?

He and Martha had spent a lot of time out here. Her house had been a hostile place to him so he had courted her on the street, holding her hand here, kissing her, postponing the moment of delivery, of handing her back to her close-watching parents. The memory of those goodnights was still sweet in his mind. A hissing sound made him turn and look for the cat.

There stood a girl in a long, brown cloak. A girl with whom he had sheltered in many doorways on other wet nights long ago. A girl who was slim and whose cheekbones were marked with a kind of pride.

"Martha?" he said. And when she held out her hand to him, a hand as it once had been with no blood under the fingernails, white fingers which had never probed other people's awful orifices, he took it and followed her. He followed her, dazed, down a curved front path, through an undergrowth of branches, through a side door which was ajar and which closed magically behind him. And on up a winding, winding staircase.

Now he was inside the room with the curved window. It was an unusual room decorated with newspapers, unornamented. There was a bed, a half-moon desk littered with papers which had been pressed down by the weight of this strange girl's body. It was her room. Enviously, he looked around. It took a kind of independence, courage, a certain freedom, to live in a room like this. There were no concessions to the ordinary or the usual or the cries of salesmen.

He imagined decorating the living room this way, taking out the small but expensive china things which were supposed to reflect their taste but which only showed that once upon a time, Martha's parents had invested money in small, expensive china things.

'How unusual,' they would say, the visitors who came to see his new decor. 'How remarkable. Really, really different. Very brave. Quite admirable.' And they would smile sweetly before they tied the straitjacket behind his back and took him to a peaceful room.

"I've been watching you," Marianne said. "You were trying to make up your mind, weren't you, whether to come to me or not? So I came to fetch you."

"I'm a very ordinary man."

"Listen. I wrote this today."

"'When comes the day I can no more make love.'"

"What on earth have you been reading?"

"Listen!"

> When comes the day I can no more make love
> But hobbling bow-legged
> Into old age
> I go,
> I will but say to all who pass me by,
> The first man and the last one are the same.

"I like that. What does it mean?"

"It means," she said, and her cloak fell away, and she pushed it over her shoulders, and she was naked, "that I think it's time to make love."

"I haven't got fifty dollars to spare."

"The first time's free."

"I like to pay my way." Backing towards the window, he knocked over a collection of dead twigs. "Your mammary glands are very nice," he said.

"Forget about your wife."

"Your pubic hair is curly."

"You sound like a school exercise book. I'll put this poem in my first volume and dedicate it to you."

"Please don't. Have you met my son, Sam?"

"Come and lie on the bed with me. At least till the storm stops. I like storms. Usually I sit in the window and watch them. The trees bending and the winds roaring and thunder rolling round. Magnificent. Elemental."

He closed his eyes because she was his daughter. She was his daughter and all the children he had seen growing up from infancy. Frantically he tried to picture a diaper (do you use Pampers to keep your baby dry?), round that lovely body and peeked to make sure there wasn't one. And he was now an evil man who chased little girls in parks in order to put his hand up their skirts. Tomorrow, or today, he might be in court. Exposed. Calumniated. Hated by all the other prisoners and found one bleak morning with sixteen knives, knives stolen from the cafeteria and specially sharpened, in his body. "If we could harness the energy of a storm," he said, "it might help with the power shortage."

"Please take your shoes off."

"What has all this to do with symbiosis?"

"Don't be obstructive. We'll talk about your work later. Besides it has everything to do with it. When you live symbiotically, everything is part of it. It's like putting everything into a meat grinder. My poems are me and so is this room and so, soon, will you be, all part of this same moment in our minds and bodies."

"Don't talk about meat grinders."

She smoothed the bedcovers.

"No, I won't take my shoes off," he said. "I'm not a . . ."

Not a monster, he was going to say. I'll go in a minute when the rain stops. Sam will let me in if I knock on his window. I have to live with myself ever after. I can get a divorce from her but not from me. There is Martha. I think one infidelity is enough. Marriage isn't a rock. It can't be incessantly battered. It can't be kicked at continuously. I came out tonight to find a criminal, not to be one.

She had put her tape recorder on; her own voice was reciting a poem about a hoax, singing it faintly to an eerie tune. From upstairs came the sound of slow but rhythmic footsteps.

"That's granny practising her dance."

Men who went to work each day wearing smart suits and shirts and ties to match . . . Men who had responsible work to do, who met at meetings in the town . . . In the giant downtown, importantly, among this generation's monuments, the skyscrapers made of gold and silver foil . . . Men of whom it was said, "He knows more about the heavy water end than any one in the business. . . ." Men who had been approached to write papers and speak to groups of professionals . . . Men who went downtown each day carrying a sense of worth and a sandwich in their briefcases . . . and the dependence of others . . . did not . . . would not . . . COULD NOT.

She was kneeling naked at his feet, taking off his shoes, lifting one leg off the ground so that he over-balanced and fell back on to the bed, while out there on the street, banshees were howling . . . And his own thirty phantoms gathered round him.

She took him as the thunder and lightning rolled and shook and flashed and rain beat against the house. He cried out but she was relentless. And in the end, as the thunder faded into the lake, and the lightning stopped brightening the whole room with its instant yellow glare, there was an almighty crashing and crackling that exploded against the wall of the house. The desk in the window rattled and the bed shook.

"Another goddam tree," Marianne said, rolling off him. "For Christ's sake. Why now? Get dressed quickly."

Cold, cruel words that left him chilled and shattered. 'I

can't go just now,' he wanted to whimper. 'Not now. Not after that.' He was silent. A whole hurt hollow feeling in his whole body. He shrivelled. She had accepted him and rejected him in the same moment. Get dressed. Go.

He was putting his shoes on when the door opened and Lilliane came in saying, "It's the old elm. Terribly sad. I shall miss it. It's stood there like a sentinel over our whole lives together and all of your childhood, Marianne. Oh! Mr. Ferrand isn't it? From number twenty-five?"

Take shorter showers. Have shallower baths. The water didn't cover his thighs. In an age of total technology, the slogans on the wall read, 'Take shallower baths'.

Bob laid his head back on the plastic pillow, product of an earlier age when every luxury was provided to encourage the bather to lounge, neck deep, reading his plastic-covered library book, resting his cocktail glass on the bath table provided; and wallow. Two minutes of the shallower bath and the front of his body was damply chilled. He rubbed himself with soap quickly and then allowed the taps to run into the bath until it was three-quarters full.

He took a sip of the whisky which, for want of a bath table, was standing on the floor at his side. The bath and the whisky might counter the effects of the soaking rain on his half-dressed body but the soap and water could not ever wash him clean.

He understood now why people were afraid of thunderstorms. On nights like this one, witches rode abroad and ironwilled nymphs created their own Walpurgisnacht out of the material to hand. And old, reliable elm trees fell down.

Comfort was here in the steam. Silence. Peace. Outside the bathroom door there was hell. Retribution awaited him. Yet surely some of that had been exacted already. Had the Paper Boy, tired of being spied on, signalled a flashing lantern to Marianne who had then come to claim him?

'Yes! I do care about Dori,' he imagined himself shouting back to Martha in reply to her first recrimination. 'No,' to the second, 'I do not know how we shall continue to live on this street unless we bind all concerned to a vow of silence.'

Sam had said, Sam, coming up from his basement room and seeing his father there, wet, half-dressed, afflicted, Sam had said nothing. Sam had said nothing and turned away to return to his den and to sleep.

And now here he was, father, husband, lover, despoiler of young girls, locked in the bathroom which had become a place separate from the rest of the house, a totally isolated cabin which touched nothing, a floating space station. Outside was only chaos and walls and glass and shavings of a crumbled world. Like the relics of a war-torn house, the bathroom with him in it stood alone. He had only to get out, to try to get into bed and lie down and sleep for a couple of hours before it was daytime again.

Sleep. A damn primitive need. Surely the machine could have been adapted to perpetual wakefulness. By now. Getting on for the twenty-first century. So sleep then. And an explanation to Sam. It was time to tell Sam what was going on out there on Chellow Street. Beyond Santa Claus. Can't you hear those other myths exploding, boy?

Sleep. And then a talk with Martha. An explanation and no guilt left after it. I did what I did because a man's gotta do what. . . For Christ's sake! Well then, for Martha some half-truths. A cleanish slate. May I have the pleasure of trying to begin this waltz again?

Lilliane had stood there looking down at her hand, perhaps wishing it was longer and paler. A tall, wasted woman with long cheekbones and a flowing, dingy, green dressing gown.

Pondering what to say, she had been unable to find words that any of her heroines might have used in this situation. The calm became terrifying and no words came to him except frivolous phrases: I am a tree doctor. I make house

95

calls. What a pretty gown.

At last, Marianne had spoken, "Mr. Ferrand is just leaving, mother." And it was said with such gentle ceremony that it roused Lilliane's deep courteous instincts so that she held out her hand and Bob backed away from her as though from a royal personage, shaking her hand and clutching his clothes and shoes to him. He staggered back down the circular staircase and out into the wet night. Only as he closed their back door did he hear a shriek behind him. Lilliane had come to life. A new storm was beginning.

The whisky glass was empty. The water was cold. He could refill both and start again. He could take baths forever until his skin was a mass of little tiny wrinkles.

'I am a man with more important things to do,' he wanted to shout out. Everybody around him wanted parts of his life or explanations and all he wanted to do was live in a room with newspaper-covered walls.

'Martha,' he would say. 'I have something to tell you. . .' And all the time he was talking she would be sorting through her bandages wondering which was the right size to use.

There was a tap on the door. A push. The door opened. The door he had thought was locked, opened.

Martha came in, her thin body showing through Elsa Kwan's black dress. "I came home early," she said, reaching for a towel. "Would you like me to dry you?"

"What is this going to mean to you?" the reporter was asking. She was a young, plump woman with stringy black hair and a tiny microphone which she held out towards him like a threat. Did no one take shorthand any more? Could no one write? Always this instant speak. Instand command: Talk into this tube! Spit in this bowl! Look in this direction! Put your fingers on this pad! WELL IT'S THE NUANCES. WE GET THE

"Perhaps you should ask Mr. Mercer," he replied.

"He sent me to see you."

"Oh. Well sit down then."

Bob didn't look at her body. He had become afraid of himself. The previously ordinary husband had been inhabited by a new and lustful demon. One glimpse of her curved thigh and before he realised it they would be screwing on the office floor. Or, more likely, in view of his recent experiences, she would be across the desk in one leap, taking off his tie and shirt and pants in a simple expert way as though he was wearing a one-piece stage suit, all front, and have him there before he could shout help.

IT'S LIKE THIS, DOCTOR, IT'S NOT FOR MYSELF BUT FOR MY FRIEND. EVERYTIME I SEE A WOMAN SHE WANTS TO GET INTO BED WITH — ER — HIM. Not for me but for a friend! Who had friends any more? There was no one whom he could tell about his current life. Mercer didn't seem to have this problem. What was it about him, about Bob Ferrand, that attracted them? Was he exuding sex? Was there a soap strong enough to wash the scent away? A deodorant that would repel rather than attract? Did these younger women take him for a father figure? Mercer might have had an answer but Bob couldn't ask the question.

A year or two ago, Mercer, in a turgid moment, had said, "You know, Ferrand, you're a good guy to work with. I mean you're efficient, reliable. All that. But I was crossing the street the other day and I had one of those flash visions — you know. I could see it in my head, the car coming too fast, me knocked down, it backed over me, the policeman bending down to catch my last words and see if I had money for the ambulance. 'Who shall we send for, sir,' he's asking. And there's me whispering, 'My friend, Ferrand.' And right there in the street, I got this sickly feeling that you're my only friend and I'm not sure I even like you. It made me want to cry."

There was work, family, people like the Weibs whom one

knew and yet did not know. People with whom, like the city, one felt familiar. That was all? Familiarity? There were enemies everywhere and yet his only friend was a man who didn't particularly like him.

"Mr. Ferrand?"

"Oh yes. Sorry. I haven't been sleeping too well lately."

"The situation's been keeping you awake?"

"What exactly have you come here to talk about?"

He realised that the machine was recording everything and waited for her to answer. Do you want to know, young, plump, lady about my hobbies, my lovelife which until lately I didn't have one of, my failure at detection. But I was cheated there. The wrong person was wearing the cloak. If I had been wearing a cloak, all might be well now. If I had worn a peaked cap and carried a magnifying glass, all might be well now. As it is, I couldn't even prevent them tampering with the invitations. A list from the Paper Boy. The mailman's ringer. A little MagicErase. A substituted name. And the Quinns would never notice. Martha, pretending otherwise, had been delighted to be invited to their party.

He had set off downtown as usual, his briefcase in his hand, his head full of the facts and figures by which he earned his living, his body a strange and alien thing. The head of a respectable man on the body of a lecher. Could it be seen? Was it noticeable? Was the dark brown suit with the narrow green stripe in fact transparent so that everyone knew and could brand him with two scarlet 'A's. The outer shell of him had drawn no sniggers as he walked into the office and no one gave him a second look. The girls were involved in what looked like a meeting to compare the quality of pantihose and, in any case, they reserved all their curtseys for the President, the capo di tutti capi. So he had reached his own office without a single incident and found this chubby girl here; the product of a journalism course at some slick college where she had been taught to ask direct questions, to use a tape recorder and to keep the interviewee to the point.

98

"The hearing recommendations. The cutbacks. My editor wants a column or two. Views from the city. That kind of thing. So I'm asking people like you — engineers, manufacturers — how it's going to affect you."

"Your machine affects me. It's difficult to be spontaneous when you know it's all being recorded."

"I thought everybody was used to that nowadays. Electronics are here to stay."

"I can only tell you obvious things. When there are project deferments, there are naturally going to be cutbacks. Layoffs."

"What do you think of the government's policy on this?"

"Shortsighted as always. They'll have to build these generating stations eventually. For the time being, they're pandering to those who think everybody should be made to live in a boring, non-working, totally green, welfare state whether they like it or not. When the time comes, and they realise they have to have the stations, the work will cost more, the material will cost more. With the kind of people we have running the province, you can't expect any better."

"This is all for the record?"

"What do you want me to do, name names? I don't give a damn what you do with it. I'm only answering your questions."

"Would the government stand to make anything out of this?"

"I'm not calling them corrupt. Only incompetent. They don't listen to the experts. They listen to the people who make most noise. Is that the way to run a country efficiently?"

"Efficiency is more important than democracy?"

"Surely you're not here to talk politics?"

"You brought it up."

"I don't want to talk about anything with that machine going all the time."

"You've given me enough," she said significantly.

Oh sure. Enough to have him carted away to some new

Arctic Labour Internment Camp for Criticism and Alien Thoughts where he would spend his time bandaging his frost-bitten feet, protecting his hard-grown vegetables from psychotic marauders and pondering that these were not his real crimes.

"Even with the cutbacks, I've got work to do." His phone rang. It was Mercer. "No I'm not telling her anything. Anyway, you sent her in here."

"Afraid of letting myself go," Mercer explained. "And we can't afford to offend the provincial government just now."

"No. Right. O.K. See you."

He hung up and looked at the girl again. Was there a way in which he might leap at her and knock the machine to the ground, erasing the tape and destroying the interview without it seeming like the prelude to a sexual assault. She had, it seemed to him, backed away and was preoccupied with buttoning her coat up tightly. LACE YOUR CORSETS UP, LADIES, HERE COMES BOB FERRAND. "I'm not . . ." he was starting to say when there was a knock on the door which opened instantly to admit two men carrying a desk.

"Where shall we put this?"

"Back where you got it."

"We were told to bring it in here."

Bob's eye was caught by a new sign on his door. Over the old Robert Ferrand, plain white and black, there was a new, ornate carved wooden label which said, 'Armand Prevost.' "They're coming?" he asked the moving men.

"They're here," one of them replied. They set the desk down in the middle of the room and left.

Bob wanted to kick the solid desk. He wanted to slam the door and drive a knife through the name plate. This was his room. His soul's place in all the city. Not at home, not on Chellow Street was there a haven that was entirely his; and his old bedroom on the farm now housed the live-in help. He wanted to run to Mercer and say, 'You can't do this', and

Mercer would mutter something about its being only tempo-rary and get on with his work. If it hadn't been for the girl, he would have gone stamping off to Mercer right away but he saw, challenging, in her eyes, the preview of a black-type para-graph: Engineer throws tantrum at invasion from Montreal office. When she had gone, he would go to Mercer, go to the boss and thump his fist down on desk after desk until some-body gave him an office of his own again.

Moments later, when the girl was halfway out of the door, a dark-haired man came in carrying a half-gallon bottle of wine and a briefcase.

"'Ello Bob," he said. "'Ope you don't mind. Should 'ave been next week. There was a mix-up. I'm bringing the wine. The wine in this province is," he made a face and spat into the waste basket, "not tolerable. Would you like some now to christen our new liaison? And the lady?"

"In the morning?" Bob asked. Wine in the morning? He saw the whole office routine crumbling about him, followed soon afterwards by the bricks and mortar of the building itself. The young woman had closed the door again and unbuttoned her coat and set the tape recorder on the desk, waiting for some reaction from him. Waiting to see him throw Armand and his wine and the heavy desk out the window. Well, she would see calm and containment; the row would come later.

"She wants the wine," Armand stated, bringing a cork-screw and three wine glasses out of his briefcase. "Imported from France, this." He raised his eyes to heaven where France was and poured the wine into the glasses.

"To us all. To this lousy city may she sink into the lake. To the lady. Eh?"

"To this lousy city," Bob echoed.

"You must be pleased to see us here," Armand said to Bob.

"Down Niagara way, we never thought of you much except as hockey players. Besides I am partly one of you."

"But you've lived here, boy and adult, for years. What

'ave you done to stop this 'appening? Like ice breaking up in the river, the country breaks up, and in this lousy city a lot of pot-faced people go about saying, "Oo needs Quebec?" They'll see 'oo needs Quebec all right. I drink the wine because my heart is breaking like the ice on the river. I'm only here to work, to keep my pension money. To this lousy city."

"To this lousy city."

We started out, if you want to begin at the beginning, young lady reporter and Armand the interloper, an army of professional people, branching out to change things, in this lousy city, to make it great. All of our cells were full of energy. Each of us was a mass of creativity and talent. We were going to do such great things as young men and women do dream of . . . Maybe the tall buildings were too much for us because now we walk along long streets, carrying our briefcases with our heads bowed, to talk to each other across polished tables. My father has filled as many bushel baskets with peaches as I have spoken words. People have enjoyed the peaches which are full of vitamins. He can look out of his back door and see a long, long stretch of land which is his. His feet can tread on his own land, his hands stroke the bark of his own trees. I used to say, 'This is my city', but it doesn't acknowledge me . . . My wife, across town, works sometimes in the hospital putting shattered people back together again and we live in a detached house with our detached children and I am sometimes an expert in my field. The gold and silver skyscrapers are very new and quite beautiful but they distort the images of everything around them. You'd think, wouldn't you, that our daily feet, give us this day our daily feet, beating the same tracks would have worn the sidewalks to a groove. . . .

The wine was a solid Beaujolais, firm as the earth, true as the moon, pure as the . . . pure as the first spring breeze somewhere out of town. A fine ripe, red Beaujolais with that touch of purple in it and a strong suggestion of that greatest of human virtues, reliability.

"I do have work to do this morning," Bob said again.

"I'm afraid I've disturbed you," the girl said.

"No, you 'aven't, yet," Armand replied.

"I suppose it is a kind of celebration."

The girl, in a voice that was like a woollen scarf being drawn through a narrow brass ring, told them she relished the wine because she was getting over an unhappy love affair so shattering at its end that she couldn't be bothered to wash her hair and had started to eat chocolates by the box-full. "I'm a slim, attractive woman really."

"We'll be friends," Armand was saying.

"Friends," Bob said, "are as rare as good wine and well-dressed women. Except you, my dear, and this wine and Armand. A friend is another self, a mirror image. A person to whom one looks for an approving reflection. Right?"

"Agreed."

"I'm very 'appy just now."

"Preserve this moment in crystal, like a paperweight. A happy-moment paperweight."

"Why are you a journalist? You should be a poet. Most of my mistresses are poets. Except one who is a singer."

"In Toronto! Mistresses! Poets! You joke!"

"There was a man once," Bob began, and they faced him, sitting there on the new desk, like children anticipating a good story. "He tried to save a little bit of this city from itself. From the evil surrounding it. He was vigilant. He tried to catch the blackmailer. He went out one wet night with a stick in his hand. But that's a story too long to tell and maybe the Paper Boy arranged that also. Who else could have known to send Elsa's dress to Martha? I only went to that bar in the first place because I was looking for a woman. . .Hey! That's not true. I didn't say that. It was because I was thirsty. After a long meeting. I wanted a drink. Really."

"The tape's gone around and around and around."

"Like the wine."

"I love my work," the girl journalist said.

"No more wine for me, Armand. I've got things to do this

morning. To play hell with whoever put you in here, things like that. Other things as well."

Bob stood up. The door opened and there was a flash of gunfire and obediently he fell to the ground. It had always been like that in games, in the orchard. To be fair one fell to the ground when shot. One acknowledged that one was dead.

"You can get up, Bobbie," the girl said. "It's only my photographer."

But he didn't hear.

Three men in white coats were walking slowly down the corridor. On a bench against a bleak wall, a woman wearing a black and white evening gown sat sobbing. When she saw the men approaching, she got up, waited a moment, clutched at her throat, breathed heavily and then rushed towards them, saying in a flat voice to the middle one, a bearded negro with fine, dedicated eyes, 'Can't anybody do anything? Doesn't anybody care?' Somewhere out of sight a clarinet was carrying a melody, badly, off-key. The men didn't answer but only looked back at the woman, shook their heads as one, and walked on, their footsteps echoing hollowly down the apparently endless hall. 'Oh God,' the woman said, and sat down again not noticing that the door behind her was opening slowly.

"For Christ's sake turn that thing off," Martha shouted.

"Shall we go into the living room," Bob said.

"Shall we dance a fucking minuet," Sam echoed, sotto voce.

"See what I mean," Dori demanded.

They picked up their coffee mugs and followed him into the living room where they hadn't lived for some time and sat down as far away from each other as possible. Bob sat on the armchair near the fireplace as though he was comfortable.

Sam's long and hairy legs were coiled round the straight Chippendale chair which he had turned back to front. Dori, clutching a dressing gown round her, a towel round her hair, squatted on the floor in a corner by the window. Martha, neat in her flowered skirt and white blouse, perched on the loveseat near the door.

Martha had been calm after she got the note telling her about Elsa. She hadn't been interested in his remarks about the Paper Boy and the milkman who was probably his minion. He had been on the verge of telling her about the mailman's ringer but a look in her eye, and the knowledge that she had access to straightjackets and padded cells and blinkers and assorted muzzles, stopped him. She had been calm and cool as though casting her mind back and remembering things which she had interpreted wrongly and to which she had responded in too pleasant ways. She had made a wrong diagnosis, misread the symptoms and had treated the patient too kindly. She hadn't once said, 'I will believe none of this unless you tell me yourself that it's true.'

"I've got some studying to do," Sam said.

"I suppose you all think I'm stupid," Dori wailed, beginning to cry again.

Bob leapt at her with his handkerchief. She brushed it aside and dabbed at her eyes with the end of the towel. "Your mother and I," he began.

"Don't tell me," Dori said, "you want me to stay at home next year instead of going to Waterloo. You don't think I'm mature. Well let me tell you something. Your precious friend Jon Weib is a pretty weird guy."

"Shut up," Sam said. "This has nothing to do with you."

"It has to do with all of us," Bob went on.

They were sitting in this room disintegrating. A family, a group, unique in its relationship, with its particular memories and codes, was dying here. Fission was taking place: The atom, when bombarded with neutrons, splits, but there is not necessarily a mushroom cloud.

There had been security in the Murrays' way of bringing up their daughter. He and Martha had tried but failed to imitate it. A street and a house and the same china ornaments were no guarantee of success. Bob wanted to close the drapes and pretend it was winter and gather the children in. It had not been his intention to leave them so soon. They were older now, not damp bundles being left by some villain on the orphanage doorstep. But yet he hadn't intended to desert them now. Dori needed still to be able to reject a proffered handkerchief for a year or two. Sam was like the Questing Beast, hard to discover. At least he was seeking out a clean and living way. In smaller communities, out of the way places, the youth of Sam's age seemed to be drinking themselves into watery graves or highway funeral pyres with a driven determination, as though a harsh god was demanding so many sacrifices a year.

Martha felt as though her loud thoughts must be battering at their eardrums and finding a way into their minds: Curses. Damnation. Was this it then? I tried to be a good wife and mother. Line from a lousy soap. Laughter all round. It is not fair. All my traditional feelings have been cut. My nerve ends are exposed. I am being deserted here. Help me somebody. Take heed from this, daughter. Go and live a roaming, ravaging life, enjoy yourself, the end will be the same. She looked at Dori the stranger and Sam the man and said, "Maybe we don't need to go into everything now, Dori's upset."

"I'll go and sit in my room and I won't be a bother to you," Dori cried, stomping across the room and on up the stairs.

"What are you wanting to say?" Sam asked. "Can't we get on with it? Are you leaving? Is mother leaving? Are you both leaving?" He was looking at them with eyes which both of them had seen staring at them in exactly that way out of a five-year-old face, a ten-year-old face, a fifteen-year-old face, and now this young man's face.

"I've been asked to go to Calgary."

"Why?"

"Now that the . . . Let's just say to save an argument that for the moment there's work there, and there isn't here."

"Are we moving then?"

"Not for the time being. Your mother's going to keep on with her work here. I'll come back for weekends, holidays."

"I guess you'll want me to look after things, then."

"The garden and things, yes."

"When are you leaving?"

'I sometimes sing in Calgary,' Elsa had said at their last casual meeting. But it was not her body that flitted across the screen of Bob's mind. That was a silhouette, the outline of a strange and mystifying young girl in a cloak. Martha, when she was young, on those carefree, party days, had worn a cloak.

They all looked up sharply at the sound of a timid knock on the front door. Sam unwound himself and went out. They sat there in silence, the two of them.

"It's the paper boy," Sam called to them. "Is there any money?"

"In my purse. In the kitchen," Martha replied.

"It was over — with Elsa."

The self-pity that had, three times today, brought tears to her eyes, welled up in her again. Why me? Now? Her parents had perhaps been right. It had been wrong to transplant this farmer's son to Chellow Street. Background tells. He couldn't even go some distance for his liaison. He had lied and made up fantastic tales about the paper boy being a man of sixty instead of making a strong men-will-be-men plea and demanding absolution. Her father would have done that.

But there had been a kind of fear in Bob's eyes all the same. Dr. Warren. Could I speak to you for a moment please? My husband is fantasizing and then too he's been having an affair with a dancer round the corner. I mean she lives round the corner. Getting home just before me in the mornings.

Leaving the children alone all night. Not caring what kind of orgies they held in the dark.

And there was the black dress, delivered by mistake. What kind of a mistake was that? "It's no use talking to me about it just now," she said.

"It's true. It was over."

"Did you think I was always counting the ceiling tiles?"

"My balls."

"What!"

"I'm glad you can be so calm."

"Calm!" she laughed. "You want to see me shred up my shirt? Eat the rug? Leave me alone!"

During the long night, she had told him that his move to Calgary would make it easy for him to clear out neatly, gradually, to come back less and less often, to start packing his things and move them a few at a time until he need no longer come back at all. She cut into small pieces his future, his safe old age, the next twenty years and then a gradual retirement surrounded by familiarity.

A charming and well-dressed young woman came into the room at that moment. Her hair shone after being blown dry with a hand-dryer. Her eyes flickered with intelligence. She looked business-like in her slacks and clean, white shirt.

"It's time for me to go," she said briskly. "I'm baby-sitting at the Kalchuks. She has to go and choose a dress for the party. Then she might meet him downtown for a drink. So I'm not sure when I'll be back. Bye then." Picking up the basket that contained her knitting and her book, Dori gave them both a kiss and left.

"The paper boy wanted to know if we were going away," Sam called from the kitchen. "I told him only Dad was, temporarily."

"What made him think we were going away?"

"I guess he saw the boxes."

Bob looked at the window and the boxes and considered the angle of vision and shook his head. There was no way the

Paper Boy could have seen into the room. Had he engineered all this? Right up to the move? Neatly getting rid of the only man on Chellow Street who knew what was going on? "I feel as though I'm on trial here," he said quietly.

"Now or ever since you came?"

Thus, in a sentence, she alienated him. She cut the present out from under him and the past as well. He had, then, always seemed like an outsider to her too. At the back of her mind she had not accepted him either. He walked over to the small high window that looked out on to the street, built with no risk of passers-by visually invading the privacy of the living room. "I could have done a lot of other things," he said.

"We all had choices."

"I could have done a lot of other things," he repeated.

"I'm sorry," she said.

And this time he let her apologize without feeling that he wanted to hit her. She was partly to blame. He hoped that for the sake of his peace of mind, he would be able in time to push at least half the blame on to her. So far he hadn't found a way.

"Perhaps it isn't quite the end of everything," she said hesitantly.

"There are the children." That was what he said instead of going across to touch her and speak softly to her. It was the phrase that came into his mind and kept him standing there by the window. He chose to take her literally and said 'there are the children' because, truly, there couldn't be an end of everything as long as those two human beings existed.

"Yes," she said, turning her head, not realising that her profile might have been perfect for a Roman coin. Not realising either that the children were not extensions of herself, profiles on smaller coins, but were whole individuals, weaned and self-reliant.

And just then Sam came back into the room and said, "Is that cake ready to eat Ma? I'll take a piece to my room. Like I said, I've got work to do." And he left them there.

Part Four

It is the depth of night. He has gone out again. I thought he might come here, to me, but he went down the street and turned left under the street light and disappeared.

Amorphous. Amorphous. Amorphous. The sound of a man walking in the dark. And my life at the moment.

They have told me, the chorus of voices, to find work, to seek life, to get in touch with reality, to be like other people, but none of them has given me a blueprint or any solid directions. I learn as much of life sitting here in the dark as they do in the daylight.

He was walking like a man about to say no, about to stand in front of her and say, 'I couldn't tell you this on the phone but the truth is, I can never see you again. I have met someone younger and better.' Click.

Marianne took the cassette out of the recorder and put it on a shelf with the others. She had a stack now of fragments which might one day be useful as a kind of living diary, parts of short stories, or as the new message. It could be the television programme of tomorrow: herself dressed in glittering, glaringly coloured garments, adapting her attitudes to the words which would be played, Voice Over, in the background while scenes appropriate to the mood would flash on and off the walls. It would be called, simply, 'Marianne'.

She climbed back on to the half-moon desk and looked out into the summer night. . . .

The Reverend Cline awoke, sweating in his air-conditioned bedroom, from a dream, a very disturbing dream: he had been lying on the ground, bound like Gulliver but not by threads, by many strands of beads, while a priest bent over him, murmuring, 'There are no beads in your church my son. Perhaps you are really one of us.'

If only they had rewarded him for his regular attendance with bits of coloured thread, pictures, candies, pennies, he might not be shaking this persistent priest from his mind now.

He longed, in his sleepy musing, to reach out his hand to the long white-sleeved arm and say, 'Yes, I am coming. I am coming,' and be translated instantly to a different future. He would wake then to a day of that parish downtown which would be his expiation. He would stay there, to carry on the work; hundreds of screaming, dirty suppliants, holding out their hands to him, stamping on him with their needy boots. 'To whom much has been given. . . .'

"I don't think you gave me quite enough," he whispered to the white-sleeved arm, unable to keep the reproach from his voice but regretting deeply that it was there.

But Rocco would understand no such need for a trade-in. After all, hadn't he been given this marvellous opportunity to pursue his studies in the Geographical Truth and to lead others along the Path? He wandered, in his drowsiness, along the path again. The sad truth was that constant revisiting of the ancient scenery gave it a tarnished look; there was nothing there in that yellow and bleached place except what the traveller carried with him. As every tour guide knew, the tourist only brought away what he had taken on the journey.

As he tossed and turned, pulling the blanket over him as his body became quickly draft-cooled, he tried to reach that other time, those other days.

Imelda had been a plain but loving girl. A perfect clergyman's wife. The future had lain clear before them. And he had escaped it, at first, with Solange and Simone and the others. Until, discovered, he had been led so far astray that there seemed to be no way back.

Downtown, in the poor, ramshackle house which would go with the parish, he could offer Imelda useful work, a chance at rehabilitation.

She might become a real person again.

He could get used to the foul breath of the poor.

There was a new kind of rose, a floribunda, which would be great for the bed behind the house.

The white-sleeved arm had gone.

Blue waves lapping on a soft shore and Jeanie . . .

The priest was coming at him, trying to take the beads.

Imelda used to wear a long brown dress in the evenings.

Maybe just two more trips then. Or three to pay off all the debts.

A nice invitation to the Quinns' party.

All things bright and beautiful. . . .

Night or day in Elsa's room, it was all the same. Outside, as he walked along the quiet streets, there had only been the distant hum of night traffic, a late bird calling out in the ravine. In this silk-lined box, the smooth voice of Annie Bream, the salesman's dream, mourned the passing of life 'the way it used to be'.

"The problem with these things is," Elsa began to say, "Look is there a bit of slip showing? At the back? Is that they get time-consuming. You know. They begin to take over. This is my night for doing the laundry. And here you are. What are you doing here?"

She was sorting out all the coloured underwear into piles of green and blue and black. The pantihose she was putting neatly into a mesh bag.

"It's very important for me to have some kind of routine. You know. For my voice. If I get too tired, I don't sing right. Last Thursday, when I was doing 'Let it be me', they said there was a guy from Worldwide there. It takes a lot out of a person. And I need my sleep. What do you think this chair looks like here?"

He crept up on her while she was gathering the black underwear into a heap. "I don't care," he said.

"You don't care about anything. The chair. My laundry. My voice."

He pushed her back into the bedroom. Onto the bed.

"I've got the machine on," she shouted, struggling against him. "It'll go through its cycle with no clothes."

"I can do that too," he replied.

"Mmmmm," she said. "Mmmmmm."

Strangely, he felt as though he was screwing three women one on top of another and Martha was at the bottom, on the bed. AM I GETTING THROUGH TO YOU MARTHA? AM I? AM I? AM I? EH? AM I?

The great throbbing hospital machine had slowed down to a steady humming noise. The huge animal was resting but vigilant. Martha had taken off her shoes and was lying on a couch in the doctors' lounge. So far it had been a quiet night. They could have managed without her. But as usual, when they had called and said, 'We need you', she had grabbed her white coat and come along to hide away out of sight of the whole world; a night person.

She didn't want to admit that she loved it here, that it was home. She liked the softness of the atmosphere, the rushed urgency when the accident cases came in and the fact that, without hesitation, she and the others could work together in those moments oblivious to personal problems.

When they went to parties, she and Bob, which was rarely now, they said to her, people she knew well but whose faces she could hardly call to mind, 'You could have so-and-so's job at the Institute. You need more time off. When were you last in Europe? You shouldn't be working so hard.' They couldn't have understood that this place had become more of a fortress to her than any Bavarian castle.

But they would go to the Quinns' party. They would both go. If she felt cold towards Bob, it need not show. She could stand beside him and be gracious, behave as though nothing had happened. What, after all, was Elsa Kwan? She represented no permanent threat.

"It will take time", she had said to him, parroting the heart-broken phrase of wronged wives everywhere. She wondered how it translated into French, into Chinese, into Gaelic, and imagined it as a multi-language echo reverberating round the world through space and time.

"I shall eventually cope," she said to herself. Elsa Kwan was a type. After Grandfather Drayton, so they said, had come back from his three week trip to Niagara Falls with a dancer from the Burlesque, he had spent the last thirty years of his life sleeping, at nights, on a short camp bed in the smallest bedroom.

Bob should not do that. This present arrangement, his nights, her days, the old warm-bed affair of immigrant workers, suited them just now. Calgary for a short time, perhaps. And sooner or later everything would be all right again. And the children would be all right. Dori, the young lady whom they had left at Waterloo had her own standards and would return to them, a loving daughter, always. Sam meanwhile held out a hand to her, as he had once, aged five, held out his hand to help her across a nasty patch of ice and both of them had fallen down.

"Dr. Ferrand," the voice murmured. "Dr. Ferrand. Mr. Brown is hemorrhaging."

"I wasn't asleep," Martha said, sitting up. "I'll be right there. Right there."

"I came to say goodbye," Bob said, not looking at Elsa as he fastened his pants and put his jacket on.

"Always the well-dressed gentleman," Elsa said, from the bed.

"I came to say goodbye," he repeated.

"I know. I know. You couldn't do it over the phone. They always say that and come back for one last screw. You know. Like it's a dividend or something. The extra cup of coffee in the jar. If one more guy says to me, 'I couldn't do it over the phone', I'll tell him where to shove it."

"I'm thinking of your career."

"Like shit you are. You're thinking of your wife. Your nice comfortable life. Your pretty house. I could've done my laundry by now."

"Well goodbye then and . . ."

"Don't say thank you," she yelled. "I was through with you anyway. There's this agent wants me to go to Florida with him in November. And sing there. And he's jealous. And he's twice your size. . . ."

Bob closed the door and crept away, knowing, for the first time in his life what it was to 'slink'. On the way home he didn't even look round for the Paper Boy who might, at this moment, be writing a note to Martha, about Marianne. It was too early for the morning delivery but someone was there, lurking in the Quinns' shrubbery, he heard them jump back as he approached.

"If people knew how fantastic the nights are they wouldn't waste them in sleep." Marianne repeated the sentence over and over again. It could not possibly be original. Perhaps a line from a tatty old song of the thirties that her mother muttered sometimes; 'It doesn't do to dissipate the moonlight'. Surely not 'dissipate'. Couldn't be that. But it had all been said. She picked the tape recorder up and turned it over wishing it was round like a football.

She heard his footsteps through the open window. Amorphousamorphous-amor. He had stayed quite long enough to make love, the bastard, and was creeping back now to his empty bed, thinking himself unseen, although he knew she watched. And waited.

Weighing the tape recorder in her hand like a stone, she drew her arm back and hurled it towards Bob. But the house was set too far back. She didn't have the distance. He didn't even notice as it landed softly inside the fence, in the shrubs. Not dancing this time. He went into his own house, opening the door with the key, and knew that he was alone, on the street, in the night and in the world.

Marianne went to bed and cried.

The Reverend Cline reached out in his dreams for the perfect hand on the end of the white-sleeved arm and found that it was a hook.

Martha had stemmed the flow. The pale, desperately sick man had asked in his delirium for a kiss. She patted his cheek and walked away. "I'll be in the lounge, nurse, if you need me."

"The bicycle is a very popular form of transportation these days."

"A lot of people seem to be riding them. Yes."

"They're a goddam nuisance if you're driving a car."

"Ah well. It's the gratings, isn't it. They have to avoid the gratings, get their wheels caught in them, so they ride out in the road and then the cars behind have to slow down."

"Why don't we have more cycle paths like in Europe?"

"And Ottawa."

It had been cloudy in the morning but the sky had cleared and the sun had come out. 'Royal Weather' for the Quinns. The high, jagged stump of the elm pointed at the sky accusingly, pots of bought flowers softened the grim appearance of the rough grass and ferns and untended shrubs. Old garden chairs had been placed about the garden enticingly in shady places. Cars were parked all round the semi-circular drive and up and down both sides of Chellow Street.

"Did you know, Quinn, that you've got a trumpet vine back here?"

"No, My wife does all the gardening."

"I see."

"How nice of you to come."

"Delighted to hear from you. It's been easily ten years."

"More like fifteen."

"Does this mean we'll be seeing you about more?"

"I'm not sure. I can't answer that at the moment. I'm dedicated to my work. Simply to BEING."

Lilliane trailed her long sleeves over the table with its white cloth, telling people to help themselves but warning them of the dangers hidden in the caterer's sausage rolls and cheese balls. She had added dulse juice to the punch as an antidote and it had turned a beautiful deep shade of green.

"Well, Johnson. I'm not sure this won't put the stock up a bit. Time for you to emerge. Brilliant idea this party. Your wife think of it?"

"Actually we read about it in the paper. Something about us thinking of having a party. So. . . For God's sake don't touch that punch. Plebeian poison! Come inside and I'll get you a real drink."

Jim Gordon had only come to the party because he wanted to see what Marianne was wearing. It turned out to be a perfectly respectable summer gown made of real, non-see-through material and the slit up the side stopped just below her ass. It was quite ordinary.

"I wouldn't advise you to drink that punch," she said, as he was reaching out for a cup of it. "Have you got something for me?"

He handed her a letter and stood still while she read it, knowing from experience that the reaction could range from a violent scream to 'how many copies are you going to print?'

She read it aloud: "'We are flattered by your interest and would of course be pleased to see anything else you write. We feel that while this particular ms. may not be exactly for us, your work has great promise. We do advise you to send your ms. to other publishers.' That means my poems are shit."

"No Marianne. Your sense of rhythm, choice of words are great. There's still this question of reaching out a bit more to life. For instance, you only write about men. There's this whole woman thing these days. A young woman like you ought to be aware of that, into it even. Why don't you try developing your relationships with women?"

Marianne's vision of a slim volume of poems with a screaming orange sun-ray cover faded. Women, he said. Was that what he was saying? Not, come and sit in this store Marianne and autograph copies of your book and be important and all the young people will want T-shirts with your name on. Not, come inside our warm and promised land and listen to people saying how great your work is. But go and get closer to women, men, life, money. Like Jack Grope, he was telling her to run away and play, Marianne, and come back when you know something. Women. Men. Money. She brushed aside a few tears and walked away moving her hips gently from side to side. It was a comfortable, easy way to walk and it was an expression, not poetic, of her new life.

Gordon was standing there, watching her go, sad, uncertain, overwhelmed by the power gathered in this garden, when a man in a tweed suit carrying a handful of papers strode violently towards him. He had to move quickly to avoid being knocked down.

"Forgive me," the man said, "I was measuring. Habit. Fine piece of real estate this. An apartment block here could have the greatest view in the city. Chellow Heights. I fancy a statue out front. A sculpture of assorted human problems. Shrubs round the base. Lit up in winter. Makes people glad to come in out of the cold."

"Are the Quinns selling?"

"Not that they know of, yet."

"Did they ask . . .?"

"I wasn't invited if that's what you're going to say. I read the papers. Always turn up at these do's. Never touch the food and drink. Poisonous usually. On the way out might drop a hint in the ear of the host. Excuse me." And he strode off, measuring the width of the property this time.

"Mr. Ferrand. I wouldn't sit there if I were you. Unless you like sitting on graves. It's supposed to be a secret. But one of these days I'll write it down. The trouble is I'm so busy with dancing engagements, I hardly ever have time to sit down."

"I'm sorry."

"It's quite all right. He was dead. Dead as a doorstop. I know you. You're the man who comes home at 5:13, then 5:23, then . . ."

"May I fetch you something to eat?"

"You want to get away from me I expect. They all say to me, 'May I fetch you something', and then they don't come back. He," she said, kicking at the stones, "did that once too often. Went to fetch me a trifle, he said, and I sat there looking forward to it. I was wearing a long gypsy skirt and blouse with tiny lace ruffles and I was going to dance the military two-step with him, after I'd eaten the trifle . . . It's wrong to expect too much from men, I suppose. It's probably the cause of a lot of deaths . . ."

'You have to come,' Martha had said to him. 'It'll look

odd otherwise.' And now here was Lilliane who had not leapt after him shrieking that night, in the rain and in her night-gown, coming straight for them wearing a dress that looked like several flame-coloured veils strung casually together.

"Granny's been entertaining you with her stories," she uttered, graciously holding out the long-sleeved arm with no sign of a hand on the end of it. His voice was dry and no sound came out of his mouth. He was in an enchanted garden with strange and unnatural women of all ages. Why were none of them screaming: Martha of betrayal? Lilliane of savagery? Marianne of his cowardice? Were they trying, by this calm carelessness, to drive him mad?

"Yes," he croaked.

"Nice of you to come," she replied. "Come along Granny. I don't think you've met Denise."

This was their way. Down where he came from there would have been shouts of rape and all bloody murder would have been let loose. Defiled daughter. Injured parents. Suddenly hunted man. But this was their way to an outsider. The quiet arrogance. They knew. You knew that they knew. One more move towards their daughter and you would find yourself cut off at the knees and left standing there. One of their own, a local boy, would have been measured according to his status (financial and social) and a deal arranged in a civilised way over whisky. (Not much water for me, please. And no ice. I'll be with you as soon as I've got my pants on.)

"Isn't this a nice party," Marianne murmured to him, having crept up on him again, cat-like. "I hope you didn't catch cold the other night. You owe me fifty dollars."

"But you said . . ."

"I changed my mind."

"Your mother seems very calm about it."

"Don't take that for granted. Why did you come?"

"My wife thought I should."

"Do you want to come inside with me? It's pretty boring out here."

"Thank you, no."

"Are you going to give me a cheque now or will you mail it?"

Resting his foot on a rock he wrote her a cheque and hoped that the other guests would think it was a donation to charity.

"Fantastic," she was saying, "isn't it? The rocks and things they're finding on Mars. Up there. So far away. That marvellous strawberry colour. Strawberries and cream. Not green cheese at all. Make it payable to Marianne Quinn Inc."

"Inc?"

"That's right. Thanks. And if you ever . . . you know. I'd make sure we weren't interrupted next time. I do care about you. I also need the money. Excuse me. Here's Henry. My analyst. Poor dear. Don't drink that punch, Henry. Come inside. I've got wine in my room."

"This is a rare treat for me," the Reverend Cline was telling his hostess. "I spend my life going to and from the airport and visiting my poor wife in hospital. This is an oasis of pleasure in my dull life."

"Dull, Reverend Cline. Come now. You're being modest. It sounds very exciting to me. I've always wanted to visit the Holy Land."

Cline looked round the garden at Lilliane Quinn's female acquaintances. They were slightly younger than his usual clientele. But they were richer and slimmer and very ripe. Maybe they could work out some kind of a deal. This ethereal lady might welcome a percentage. Rocco might welcome the Quinn name.

"I can't tell you," he said, "of the very deep spiritual gratification to be gained by standing where He once stood, and breathing the air where He once was. By treading those same paths and touching the very stones. People return from my trips with a changed outlook, a new grasp of life. But I'm sure you have enough satisfaction in your own life to want to come on one of my little excursions."

"I'm not sure, Reverend Cline. There's the money . . ." she glanced wistfully at the house. "Of course, now that Marianne's working."

"I might be able to give you a cut-rate. Perhaps we can go somewhere quiet and talk about it."

Marianne was sitting cross-legged on her bed watching Henry the analyst zip up his fly. She was watching him happily, steeped in the new awareness of her own existence, of a loss of awe, an intimate, reflective delight. For three years he had been God and rule-maker. In fact he was a lesser man than Bob Ferrand who pretended no superior knowledge and was even diffident.

"This is a social occasion, Marianne," Henry was telling her crossly. "We are meant to mix with people. Chat to them. Make them feel at home. Make them feel they did you a favour by coming here today. They have to make you feel you did them an honour by asking them. That's what a party is. Now let's see how you can manage that."

"You owe me fifty dollars," she said to him. "Cash or a cheque. I operate on a pay-as-you-go basis."

"So nice of you to come," Marianne announced, walking like a princess towards Elsa, holding out her hand. "Did we invite you?"

Elsa was clinging to the arm of a much older man who now said proudly, "Mrs. Kwan is with me."

"Our lover is over there," Marianne whispered to Elsa, pointing at Bob. But Elsa only looked at her new love and drew him away, hinting that the daughter had always been strange, like the grandmother and it was just as well they kept them shut away in this huge house.

Martha admired the flowers and walked once round the outside of the house; inside it would be cobwebs and a stronger smell of death and mice running wild on the floors. The front door was open but all that could be seen was a hall table with a starchy flower arrangement on it, and a wide staircase down which Granny was tripping side to side, step to step. She was wearing a long, red skirt and carrying a black fan from which feathers dangled in strings to the ground.

"Why not dance for us first?" two of the Quinn cousins were asking, leading her towards the library.

Other families had their problems too. Martha backed away. She wished she hadn't come. It was not, as she had pretended to Bob, politeness which had made her accept this invitation. Nor was it any great thing for her to be able to tell her colleagues that she had spent the early evening at the home of the Quinns. None of them would care. She had really come out of nostalgic curiosity. She wanted to lift a curtain, look back into that other world and make sure that it was still the same. Against all her belief and knowledge, she willed it to be still the same.

Looking around her she saw distorted images and human beings out of focus drifting about the foliage carrying glasses of that appalling green stuff. They were making the same gestures, saying the same phrases as those people from that other, dimly remembered world.

She took another sip of the punch. It was a relaxing afternoon. As she watched, the edges of the people and the house itself dissolved and became firm again. The same thing happened to her. It was a softening, a real physical feeling. She wanted suddenly to pick small flowers and sway to gentle romantic tunes. After all, he had not been of their kind. He had, without complaint, taken on her and her ways and her people and brought the children up according to her rules. This one small fling was nothing. It would never happen again.

She should have met him at the door occasionally wearing a string bikini. A new perfume would excite him. She hitched up her skirt, turning it over at the top so that it touched her knees. Let fashion go to hell. She must find him and talk to him. She tried to pick him out in the crowd. 'I shall be wary,' she would say to him, 'but I shall be loving.'

Alva Soper was coming towards her just as Alva Soper's mother might have come towards her mother, a question already framed to ask. But the newspaper lady beat her to it and stood over them both, gushing words, "Dr. Ferrand is it? My what a charming outfit. I'll call it Black and Orange surprise. Is your husband here, Mrs. Soper? I don't see him. It is the current Mrs. Soper, isn't it? I get you all mixed up. I think there's another of you here somewhere. I was just talking to our charming hostess. How delightful of her to open up this lovely place again. Why do you think they've kept it to themselves for so long? One hears the most intriguing stories but my editor has a fixation about facts. At least three-quarters facts! That's why I get stuck with things like Black and Orange surprise and the fourth Mrs. Soper. It is the fourth, isn't it? I see little Mariana's analyst over there. Does he live here? They let granny out of her straitjacket for a time too. How nice. Even Johnson is keeping on his feet for the occasion. Great to have the sunshine. I was in Nice last week with the Bruzzi's. They spend most of the year there now. Have you visited them? Such charming people. Chellow Street used to be a lovely street but all kinds of people have moved in. Kind of the Quinns not to be suing your husband, Dr. Ferrand. After Lilliane found him practically raping the girl."

'Stop!' Martha wanted to yell but though her mouth was open, no words came out of it.

"But you seem to have sorted it out in a nice neighbourly way and my editor won't let me touch it."

"You", Martha tried to say but it came out as "Ugh".

The woman went on, her eyes searching the garden like a lighthouse beam, "Is that the Moxfords over there? What did the Quinns do? Push invitations under the door addressed to Occupant? I must speak to her. Such a character. Says the cutest things. No class at all. And is that long, long thing really a mink stole? In this weather? Must go and chat to them. See you."

Martha saw Bob standing quietly by himself. A moment ago she had seen him writing something for the Quinn girl. Something that looked like a cheque. She turned cold and then hot again. They would have to go home. There would have to be a final severing of this woman and that man. She wanted to scream at him, here in the garden. She took a step towards him and found Lilliane at her elbow, looking intently at her.

Bob was looking at all the finely dressed women. They were not his type. Most of them were so self-assured that surely nothing would ever disturb them. Maybe in their rooms, late at night, they took off their eyelashes, wiped off the make-up, let the masks slip, allowed their emotions to take over and spent the night in a kind of howling catharsis so that the next day they would be calm again and beautiful. His head was beginning to ache and he wished he had worn a hat.

He wanted nothing more now than to go home with Martha and have a cup of tea with her and to sit there talking in a rambling sort of way about the children. He wanted to find her and take hold of her hand and say, 'Please, take me home.' All these sexual excursions had been journeys into a void. Nothing good had come of sex.

One of the women was coming towards him now.

"I don't think we've met," she said.

"I'd have remembered," he replied, wondering where he had cribbed that line and chalking himself up one point for charm.

"I'm Althea Elliot, a vague relation of Johnson's. You must be a neighbour."

"How can you tell? Do I have neighbour marks?"

She shrieked with laughter and he chalked himself up another point for wit.

"Marvellous," she cried. "Say something else. Come and meet my husband. No one ever, ever says original things any more."

Green slime had replaced the blood in his veins; it was no longer a nice, wine-red liquid but a slow, oozing fluid and he caught sight of Martha standing near the shrubbery with Lilliane, deep, as people always say, in conversation, not shallow but 'deep' in conversation. It had been affected by the sunlight, synthesized, all that green slime, and it was beginning to bubble lightly in his body. Marianne was not a minor; she was twenty if a day and would not lie (or would she?) in the witness box; Martha it wasn't me, it was a damn great tree crashing down, you can see the stump of it there.

"Look," Althea was bawling at him, "you must come to my party next week."

He pushed her out of his way and dodged behind a tree to avoid the tangible iron glance that was coming his way from the two women.

Martha left Lilliane. What use were apologies? What use ritual politeness? She said to Bob, "I should have known what you were like," and, even in her fury, was ashamed of the loudness of her voice.

"I thought — she looked like — you were the same once," he called back, running to the side to dodge her oncoming anger and slipping in something green and nasty.

"My mother was right," she yelled at him, moving sideways to keep in line with him.

"She was a narrow-minded old bitch," he shouted and saw that he had disturbed the Reverend Cline who was throwing up on the rockery.

"That kind," the Reverend Cline said, wiping his mouth, "often make the best wives."

"And so am I. So am I 'narrow-minded' about some things," Martha hollered.

"I know. Martha . . ." he pleaded, hoping for a moment that the mention of her name would erase this scene and wind back the tape.

"What fun," Althea shouted. "You must BOTH come to my party next week. Really original people."

Bob tried to move backwards but the rocks stopped him. He could turn and flee but where to? At some point he would have to go home for his toothbrush.

"I can explain everything," he shouted at the top of his voice.

"I expect you can," she said, not needing to shout. She was close now, close. He saw that her face was contorted in eternal rage because she knew everything, because they had made a scene in public, and there would be no redemption for him this side of the marriage bed.

Bob stumbled on a rock. He reached out for Martha and fell into her arms.

Early orange leaves were drifting down on to Chellow Street. In a week or two, the city works department would be sending trucks and small bulldozers to scoop up the leaves and to gather information for the Paper Boy. On their way to and from the central compost heap, the vehicles would loosen the foundations of these solid houses and dent the cars parked beside the road.

In a few MORE weeks, the weather would be cool and now and then a few flakes of snow might fall among leaves. Those first flakes heralded the freezing winter when Chellow Street became narrower and narrower, and every driveway not salted or sprinkled with sand was a hazard to human limb, when the demonic winter machinery was unleashed to chase

the unwary pedestrian, and flowers wilted and turned yellow
and shrubs were shrouded in green plastic to protect them
from bitter winds and ice.

Meanwhile, the temperature was still twenty-five degrees
Celsius and the Reverend Cline, up early, his inner time clock
always out of kilter, was sitting in his garden, wearing his
round panama hat and reflecting on the forces that shape the
lives of unobtrusive men.

He heard a door open and saw Ferrand come out, alone.
He was leaving then. His behaviour at the party had been
attributed to drunkenness which was not a crime on Chellow
Street. The Reverend Cline found himself standing up, he
found that he had removed his hat and was holding it at his
side. No one was playing *O Canada*. He was standing there, rig-
idly, in a one-man salute. Ferrand was leaving, getting out,
going away: and he, Cline, was setting off next day on another
tour of the Holy Land. As he sat down again in his garden
chair, the Reverend Cline felt his eyes water. He wanted to
throw up but there was nothing inside him at all.

Out of the corner of his eye, Bob could see the Reverend
Cline but did not turn to speak to him. He was laden down
with burdens in any case and wanted no conversation, particularly not sanctimonious claptrap.

Sam would have helped him to carry the stuff down the
road but classes had started. The boy had adopted a kindly
attitude towards both his parents, laying no blame, certainly
not considering the acceptance of any. He had wished Bob
well, promised to look after Martha, picked up his bag of
books and gone.

Dori was already in Waterloo. They had driven her
there, stopped for dinner on the way, pretended amiable and
pleasant family conversation, and left her in the Student Village with its poster on the wall proclaiming, 'Jesus loves you',
and where she was now, no doubt, prey to all kinds of freaks
and revolutionaries. He and Martha had driven home in
silence.

And in silence now he was leaving. Martha had decided

to keep on working at the hospital. At least for a few more months. One got caught up in Emergency, she said. There was a kind of urgency of life and death and certain things that seemed to matter. She had become a small, white cocoon. Untouchable.

'I shall be all right,' she had stated, accepting her role as woman and not even considering that he might be the one who was not all right. Men were supposed to leap away from such ties as home and family with satyr-like delight and not look back.

'You'll like this little apartment,' the company agent had told him, 'it has beautiful parquet floors.' But he had not given any instructions as to what might be done when footprints (the tracks of the many beautiful young maidens who would scent that there was a new, unattached man in the city) and shifting furniture had rendered the parquet floors unlovely.

The airport limousine could only come as far as the barricades on the Chellow Street cul-de-sac. Outside the Moxfords', Bob stopped to move his skis to the other shoulder and to hang his flight bag on them. Was she in there now, lying on the stole, watching the morning shows on T.V.? Had she squeezed oranges for her husband's breakfast? Did the roots from his peach tree struggle to force their way up through her floor?

He hadn't liked to ask whether he would be able to see the Rockies from the apartment window. The importance of it would have escaped them.

He looked back down the street. The Quinn house was spread against the end there, sentinel and giant.

Knowing that he was going, Martha had stayed upstairs and was not watching. 'My husband's in Calgary.' 'My husband's in Timbuctu.' Sam had said, 'When you sell the house.' Dori had gone. A surge of anger that seemed to come up out of the swampy ground on which the house was built, rose up in her. To avoid the trap she had gone out and sought a husband from elsewhere and had worked hard at a profession that was, face it truthfully, menial. She had brought up two children with dutiful care and had not paid undue attention to material things. And all the time she had been living inside the goddam trap itself, driving willingly into the cul-de-sac and letting the string be drawn tight after she was in the bag. With a cry of torment, she picked up a Danish figurine, a peaceful child sleeping, bought by her mother on one of her trips abroad forty-five years ago for the nursery, and hurled it to the ground.

The Paper Boy drove down Lippert Boulevard in his Mercedes and slowed down to wave to Bob graciously. It was a winner's wave.

Bob watched the square end of the car disappear out of sight.

He looked at his own house. She was not watching but had stayed out of the way, waiting quietly for him to leave.

Nobody had sawn down the broken trunk of the dead elm in front of the Quinn castle. Blind like the mythical giant, it saw nothing of the danger that was creeping towards it. He had tried to tell them all. None of them cared.

A hand appeared at the window of the round tower and he waved back.

'Why Marianne?' Martha had cried at him. 'It's like taking advantage of a mongoloid girl or something. How could you. I realise now that I don't know you at all. Men change at your age. But not that much.' So he had been a monster all along, maliciously hiding his fangs and cleft feet for over twenty years. Her parents had been able to see the truth and had gone to live as far away as possible, out of sight and hearing of any unnameable crimes he might commit. And had now committed.

Watching him leave, Marianne felt a tug of regret. She wasn't sure what had driven him away. Only, seeing him sometimes, going down the street at strange times, he had acted as though pursued by malignant demons. He was not like the animal men Jack Grope introduced to her. Bob Ferrand was gentle with an inner core of poetry in him. He was a man with whom one could have sat forever watching waves on the shoreline rippling over the sand and receding again. He belonged perhaps in the orchards of his childhood and would never be able to find his way back to them. She reached for a pencil and her notebook. The street was closed off. He was having to carry everything down to the corner. The least she could do was immortalise his departure.

"Our lover is leaving," Marianne said to Elsa, writing down the words as her title. "Did he pay you very much?"

"I did it for love," Elsa replied.

"Don't we all, all the time?" Marianne asked, looking out of the window again. "He did. When he made love, great trees came crashing down. And there was lightning and thunder."

"He seemed fairly ordinary to me."

"My mother is so glad that I've got a female friend to stay while she goes away. She's leaving on Friday. Would you like to hear what I wrote about it? 'Following another route, We reach the same ecstatic end. . . .' "

"Shut up and come back to bed."

If Bob had known an effective curse, he might have directed it like a thunderbolt towards the Quinn house. A curse on the dead Giant and his forefathers who had struggled from places like Poland and Germany and Scotland to fight the wilderness and had only left behind a generation of namedroppers and do-gooders and decadents. A curse on them all because they had produced these ineffectual great-grandchildren who were allowing the city to be run by a series of committees; all areas of operation were now guided by young smooth-faced lawyers and economists (puppets of the Paper Boy) who explained their ill-informed views to sleepy politicians and all their resolutions were carried as read or said. The gold and silver skyscrapers of which Gerald had built the foundations would crumble before long and the whole city disappear into its own quagmire. This place, in a hundred years, might be a vast peach orchard.

At the corner of Lippert Boulevard, Bob stood the skis on end and rested his case down. He was ten minutes early.

The Boss who was only, after all, the Paper Boy wearing an inscrutable slant-eyed mask, had said, 'You'll do well in Calgary.' Mercer had offered him the sop of envy, painting a glowing picture of snow-capped mountains, electric blue sky and great steaks. A new start. A new way of life. And the continuing Stivel project. A chance to be in at the beginning.

A strange feeling round his feet made him look down. At the same time a voice called, "Hey. Get off there. We're coming to roll it. It's wet. Can't you see the sign?"

His feet and skis came reluctantly up from the wet cement. His suitcase had left a deeper imprint.

"Look at this. It's drying. Didn't you see the sign?"

"I'm sorry," Bob said.

He crossed to the other corner and tried to wipe the cement off the ends of his skis before it dried. The boy with the broken legs was sitting on his skate board moving it with his hips from side to side down the curb and across the road with a slick skill. He was shut out from school, two broken legs being considered too great a handicap, so he moved around the street alone, on his wheels.

"Snowing up North is it?" the boy asked.

"No. I'm moving out."

The mailman's ringer looked at him and his skis curiously. He was on his way to deliver a new box of lightbulbs to Mrs. Blue. The management of the store had apologized humbly for the damage done to her garden. The demonstration of their new model had been intended for another house on another street. Anything they could do to replace her garden would be done. So far they had sent her nine boxes of lightbulbs, and every time she phoned, hysterically, to complain, they sent her more.

Bob toyed with the idea of explaining to this child beside

him all the intricacies of the conspiracy, to tell him about the Paper Boy. Someone should know. Someone should fight back. But he looked again at the street and its barricades, at the mailman's ringer and Mrs. Blue, at the stone and brick houses with their defiant pillars and porches, at the ugly townhouse, and at his own house with the note inside, the one he had left on the table, hoping that there would be no answer 'Back at Thanksgiving for boots and poles'; and he figured that Chellow Street would make a good orchard. "You'll get yours," he said softly.

The limousine was approaching. He could see it far down the road. He listened for a moment. Was there going to be a last-minute bugle call, a band of merry men to his rescue, a hand reaching out to snatch him from the tumbril?

He moved the skis and suitcase to the edge of the sidewalk. The boy scooted over to him, crabwise. "Keep an eye on these, please," Bob said to him. The workmen had gone back to their coffee. He walked over and placed his foot firmly in the cement. At least he would leave something on Chellow Street.

Footprint.
R.F. 1976.